The Tales Of The Heptameron

Vol. III

by

Margaret, Queen Of Navarre

Double9 BOOKS

The Tales Of The Heptameron
Vol. III

by Margaret, Queen Of Navarre

ISBN: 978-93-70814-60-8

Published by

DOUBLE 9 BOOKS

2/13-B, Ansari Road
Daryaganj, New Delhi – 110002
info@double9books.com
www.double9books.com
Tel. 011-40042856

ABOUT THE AUTHOR

Marguerite de Navarre (1492–1549) was a prominent French princess, Queen of Navarre, and Duchess of Alençon and Berry. Born into the powerful House of Valois, she was the daughter of Charles, Count of Angoulême, and Louise of Savoy. Marguerite was married to Henry II of Navarre, and her influential position in the French court allowed her to have a significant cultural and political impact. Known for her intelligence, wit, and patronage of the arts, Marguerite was an important figure during the Renaissance. She was also a writer, best known for her collection The Heptameron, a work that reflects her interest in both literature and human experiences, exploring themes such as love, fidelity, and social norms. Marguerite's life also intertwined with various religious and political movements of her time, and she played an active role in supporting the reformation in France, despite her Catholic background. Throughout her life, she balanced her duties as a queen with her literary pursuits, leaving a lasting legacy both as a ruler and a writer. Her influence extended beyond the royal court, earning her a respected place in French history. Her parents were Charles, Count of Angoulême, and Louise of Savoy.

CONTENTS

SECOND DAY—CONTINUED

TALE XIX

Pauline, being in love with a gentleman no less than he was with her, and finding that he, because forbidden ever again to speak with her, had entered the monastery of the Observance, gained admittance for her own part into the convent of St. Clara, where she took the veil; thus fulfilling the desire she had conceived to bring the gentleman's love and her own to a like ending in respect of raiment, condition and manner of life. (1)

In the time of the Marquis of Mantua, (2) who had married the sister of the Duke of Ferrara, there lived in the household of the Duchess a damsel named Pauline, who was greatly loved by a gentleman in the Marquis's service, and this to the astonishment of every one; for being poor, albeit handsome and greatly beloved by his master, he ought, in their estimation, to have wooed some wealthy dame, but he believed that all the world's treasure centred in Pauline, and looked to his marriage with her to gain and possess it.

1 The incidents related in this tale appear to have taken place at Mantua and Ferrara. M. de Montaiglon, however, believes that they happened at Lyons, and that Margaret laid the scene of her story in Italy, so that the personages she refers to might not be identified. The subject of the tale is similar to that of the poem called L'Amant rendu Cordelier à l'Observance et Amour, which may perhaps have supplied the Queen of Navarre with the plot of her narrative.—M. and Ed.

2 This was John Francis II. of Gonzaga, who was born in 1466, and succeeded his father, Frederic I., in 1484. He took an active part in the wars of the time, commanding the Venetian troops when Charles VIII. invaded Italy, and afterwards supporting Ludovico Sforza in the defence of Milan. When Sforza abandoned the struggle against France, the Marquis of Mantua joined the French king, for whom he acted as viceroy of Naples. Ultimately, however, he espoused the cause of the Emperor Maximilian, when the latter was at war with Venice in 1509, and being surprised and defeated while camping on the island of La Scala, he fled in his shirt and hid himself in a field, where, by the treachery of a peasant who had promised him secrecy, he was found and taken prisoner. By the advice of Pope Julius II., the Venetians set him at liberty after he had undergone a year's imprisonment. In 1490 John Francis married Isabella d'Esté, daughter of Hercules I. Duke of Ferrara, by whom he had several children. He died at Mantua in March 1519, his widow surviving him until 1539. Among the many dignities acquired by the Marquis in the course of his singularly chequered life was that of gonfalonier of the Holy Church, conferred upon him by Julius II.—L. and En.

The Marchioness, who desired that Pauline should through her favour make a more wealthy marriage, discouraged her as much as she could from wedding the gentleman, and often hindered the two lovers from talking together, pointing out to them that, should the marriage take place, they would be the poorest and sorriest couple in all Italy. But such argument as this was by no means convincing to the gentleman, and though Pauline, on her side, dissembled her love as well as she could, she none the less thought about him as often as before.

With the hope that time would bring them better fortune, this love of theirs continued for a long while, during which it chanced that a war broke out (3) and that the gentleman was taken prisoner along with a Frenchman, whose heart was bestowed in France even as was his own in Italy.

3 This would be the expedition which Louis XII. made into Italy in 1503 in view of conquering the Kingdom of Naples, and which was frustrated by the defeats that the French army sustained at Seminara, Cerignoles, and the passage of the Garigliano.—D.

Finding themselves comrades in misfortune, they began to tell their secrets to one another, the Frenchman confessing that his heart was a fast prisoner, though he gave not the name of its prison-house. However, as they were both in the service of the Marquis of Mantua, this French gentleman knew right well that his companion loved Pauline, and in all friendship for him advised him to lay his fancy aside. This the Italian gentleman swore was not in his power, and he declared that if the Marquis of Mantua did not requite him for his captivity and his faithful service by giving him his sweetheart to wife, he would presently turn friar and serve no master but God. This, however, his companion could not believe, perceiving in him no token of devotion, unless it were that which he bore to Pauline.

At the end of nine months the French gentleman obtained his freedom, and by his diligence compassed that of his comrade also, who thereupon used all his efforts with the Marquis and Marchioness to bring about his marriage with Pauline. But all was of no avail; they pointed out to him the poverty wherein they would both be forced to live, as well as the unwillingness of the relatives on either side; and they forbade him ever again to speak with the maiden, to the end that absence and lack of opportunity might quell his passion.

Finding himself compelled to obey, the gentleman begged of the Marchioness that he might have leave to bid Pauline farewell, promising that he would afterwards speak to her no more, and upon his request being granted, as soon as they were together he spoke to her as follows:—

"Heaven and earth are both against us, Pauline, and hinder us not only from marriage but even from having sight and speech of one another. And by laying on us this cruel command, our master and mistress may well boast of having with one word broken two hearts, whose bodies, perforce, must henceforth languish; and by this they show that they have never known love or pity, and although I know that they desire to marry each of us honourably and to worldly advantage,—ignorant as they are that contentment is the only true wealth,—yet have they so afflicted and angered me that never more can I do them loyal service. I feel sure that had I never spoken of marriage they would not have shown themselves so scrupulous as to forbid me from speaking to you; but I would have you know that, having loved you with a pure and honourable love, and wooed you for what I would fain defend against all others, I would rather die than change my purpose now to your dishonour. And since, if I continued to see you, I could not accomplish so harsh a penance as to restrain myself from speech, whilst, if being here I saw you not, my heart, unable to remain void, would fill with such despair as must end in woe, I have resolved, and that long since, to become a monk. I know, indeed, full well that men of all conditions may be saved, but would gladly have more leisure for contemplating the Divine goodness, which will, I trust, forgive me the errors of my youth, and so change my heart that it may love spiritual things as truly as hitherto it has loved temporal things. And if God grant me grace to win His grace, my sole care shall be to pray to Him without ceasing for you; and I entreat you, by the true and loyal love that has been betwixt us both, that you will remember me in your prayers, and beseech Our Lord to grant me as full a measure of steadfastness when I see you no more, as he has given me of joy in beholding you. Finally, I have all my life hoped to have of you in wedlock that which honour and conscience allow, and with this hope have been content; but now that I have lost it and can never have you to wife, I pray you at least, in bidding me farewell, treat me as a brother, and suffer me to kiss you."

When the hapless Pauline, who had always treated him somewhat rigorously, beheld the extremity of his grief and his uprightness, which, amidst all his despair, would suffer him to prefer but this moderate request, her sole answer was to throw her arms around his neck, weeping so bitterly that speech and strength alike failed her, and she swooned away in his embrace. Thereupon, overcome by pity, love and sorrow, he must needs swoon also, and one of Pauline's companions, seeing them fall one on one side and one on the other, called aloud for aid, whereupon remedies were fetched and applied, and brought them to themselves.

Then Pauline, who had desired to conceal her love, was ashamed at having shown such transports; yet were her pity for the unhappy gentleman a just excuse. He, unable to utter the "Farewell for ever!" hastened away with heavy heart and set teeth, and, on entering his apartment, fell like a lifeless corpse upon his bed. There he passed the night in such piteous lamentations that his servants thought he must have lost all his relations and friends, and whatsoever he possessed on earth.

In the morning he commended himself to Our Lord, and having divided among his servants what little worldly goods he had, save a small sum of money which he took, he charged his people not to follow him, and departed all alone to the monastery of the Observance, (4) resolved to take the cloth there and never more to quit it his whole life long.

4 The monastery of the Observance here referred to would appear to be that at Ferrara, founded by Duke Hercules I., father of the Marchioness of Mantua. The name of "Observance" was given to those conventual establishments where the rules of monastic life were scrupulously observed, however rigorous they might be. The monastery of the Observance at Ferrara belonged to the Franciscan order, reformed by the Pope in 1363.—D. and L.

The Warden, who had known him in former days, at first thought he was being laughed at or was dreaming, for there was none in all the land that less resembled a Grey Friar than did this gentleman, seeing that he was endowed with all the good and honourable qualities that one would desire a gentleman to possess. Albeit, after hearing his words and beholding the tears that flowed (from what cause he knew not) down his face, the Warden compassionately took him in, and very soon afterwards, finding him persevere in his desire, granted him the cloth: whereof tidings were brought to the Marquis and Marchioness, who thought it all so strange that they could scarcely believe it.

Pauline, wishing to show herself untrammelled by any passion, strove as best she might to conceal her sorrow, in such wise that all said she had right soon forgotten the deep affection of her faithful lover. And so five or six months passed by without any sign on her part, but in the meanwhile some monk had shown her a song which her lover had made a short time after he had taken the cowl. The air was an Italian one and pretty well known; as for the words, I have put them into our own tongue as nearly as I can, and they are these:—

What word shall be
Hers unto me,
When I appear in convent guise
Before her eyes?

Ah! sweet maiden,
Lone, heart-laden,
Dumb because of days that were;
When the streaming
Tears are gleaming
'Mid the streaming of thy hair,
Ah! with hopes of earth denied thee,
Holiest thoughts will heavenward guide thee
To the hallowing cloister's door.
What word shall be, &c.

What shall they say,
Who wronged us, they
Who have slain our heart's desire,
Seeing true love
Doth flawless prove,
Thus tried as gold in fire?
When they see my heart is single,

Their remorseful tears shall mingle,
Each and other weeping sore.
What word shall be, &c.

And should they come
To will us home,
How vain were all endeavour!
"Nay, side by side,
"We here shall bide
"Till soul from soul shall sever.
"Though of love your hate bereaves us
"Yet the veil and cowl it leaves us,
"We shall wear till life be o'er."
What word shall be, &c.

And should they move
Our flesh to love
Once more the mockers, singing
Of fruits and flowers
In golden hours
For mated hearts upspringing;
We shall say: "Our lives are given,
Flower and fruit, to God in Heaven,
Who shall hold them evermore."
What word shall be, &c.

O victor Love!
Whose might doth move
My wearied footsteps hither,
Here grant me days
Of prayer and praise,
Grant faith that ne'er shall wither;
Love of each to either given,
Hallowed by the grace of Heaven,
God shall bless for evermore.
What word shall be, &c.

Avaunt Earth's weal!

Its bands are steel
To souls that yearn for Heaven;
Avaunt Earth's pride!
Deep Hell shall hide
Hearts that for fame have striven.
Far be lust of earthly pleasure,
Purity, our priceless treasure,
Christ shall grant us of His store.
What word shall be, &c.

Swift be thy feet,
My own, my sweet,
Thine own true lover follow;
Fear not the veil,
The cloister's pall
Keeps far Earth's spectres hollow.
Sinks the fire with fitful flashes,
Soars the Phoenix from his ashes,
Love yields Life for evermore.
What word shall be, &c.

Love, that no power
Of dreariest hour,
Could change, no scorn, no rage,
Now heavenly free
From Earth shall be,
In this, our hermitage.
Winged of love that upward, onward,
Ageless, boundless, bears us sunward,
To the heavens our souls shall soar.
What word shall be, &c.

On reading these verses through in a chapel where she was alone, Pauline began to weep so bitterly that all the paper was wetted with her tears. Had it not been for her fear of showing a deeper affection than was seemly, she would certainly have withdrawn forthwith to some hermitage, and never have looked upon a living being again; but her native discretion moved her to dissemble for a little while longer. And although she was now resolved to leave the world entirely, she feigned the very opposite, and so altered her countenance, that in company she was altogether unlike her real self. For five or six months did she carry this secret purpose in her heart, making a greater show of mirth than had ever been her wont.

But one day she went with her mistress to the Observance to hear high mass, and when the priest, the deacon and the sub-deacon came out of the vestry to go to the high altar, she saw her hapless lover, who had not yet fulfilled his year of novitiate, acting as acolyte, carrying the two vessels covered with a silken cloth, and walking first with his eyes upon the ground. When Pauline saw him in such raiment as did rather increase than diminish his comeliness, she was so exceedingly moved and disquieted, that to hide the real reason of the colour that came into her face, she began to cough. Thereupon her unhappy lover, who knew this sound better than that of the cloister bells, durst not turn his head; still on passing in front of her he could not prevent his eyes from going the road they had so often gone before; and whilst he thus piteously gazed on Pauline, he was seized in such wise by the fire which he had considered well-nigh quelled, that whilst striving to conceal it more than was in his power, he fell at full length before her. However, for fear lest the cause of his fall should be known, he was led to say that it was by reason of the pavement of the church being broken in that place.

When Pauline perceived that the change in his dress had not wrought any change in his heart, and that so long a time had gone by since he had become a monk, that every one believed her to have forgotten him, she resolved to fulfil the desire she had conceived to bring their love to a like ending in respect of raiment, condition and mode of life, even as these had been akin at the time when they abode together in the same house, under the same master and mistress. More than four months previously she had carried out all needful measures for taking the veil, and now, one morning she asked leave of the Marchioness to go and hear mass at the convent of Saint Clara, (5) which her mistress granted her, not knowing the reason of her request. But in passing by the monastery of the Grey Friars, she begged the Warden to summon her lover, saying that he was her kinsman, and when they met in a chapel by themselves, she said to him:—

5 There does not appear to have been a church of St. Clara at Mantua, but there was one attached to a convent of that name at Ferrara.—M. and D.

"Had my honour suffered me to seek the cloister as soon as you, I should not have waited until now; but having at last by my patience baffled the slander of those who are more ready to think evil than good, I am resolved to take the same condition, raiment and life as you have taken. Nor do I inquire of what manner they are; if you fare well, I shall partake of your welfare, and if you fare ill, I would not be exempt. By whatsoever path you are journeying to Paradise I too would follow; for I feel sure that He who alone is true and perfect, and worthy to be called Love, has drawn us to His service by means of a virtuous and reasonable affection, which He will by His Holy Spirit turn wholly to Himself. Let us both, I pray you, put from us the perishable body of the old Adam, and receive and put on the body of our true Spouse, who is the Lord Jesus Christ."

The monk-lover was so rejoiced to hear of this holy purpose, that he wept for gladness and did all that he could to strengthen her in her resolve, telling her that since the pleasure of hearing her words was the only one that he might now seek, he deemed himself happy to dwell in a place where he should always be able to hear them. He further declared that her condition would be such that they would both be the better for it; for they would live with one love, with one heart and with one mind, guided by the goodness of God, whom he prayed to keep them in His hand, wherein none can perish. So saying, and weeping for love and gladness, he kissed her hands; but she lowered her face upon them, and then, in all Christian love, they gave one another the kiss of hallowed affection.

And so, in this joyful mood Pauline left him, and came to the convent of Saint Clara, where she was received and took the veil, whereof she sent tidings to her mistress, the Marchioness, who was so amazed that she could not believe it, but came on the morrow to the convent to see Pauline and endeavour to turn her from her purpose. But Pauline replied that she, her mistress, had had the power to deprive her of a husband in the flesh, the man whom of all men she had loved the best, and with that she must rest content, and not seek to sever her from One who was immortal and invisible, for this Was neither in her power nor in that of any creature upon earth.

The Marchioness, finding her thus steadfast in her resolve, kissed her and left her, with great sorrow.

And thenceforward Pauline and her lover lived such holy and devout lives, observing all the rules of their order, that we cannot doubt that He whose law is love told them when their lives were ended, as He had told Mary Magdalene: "Your sins are forgiven, for ye have loved much;" and doubtless He removed them in peace to that place where the recompense surpasses all the merits of man.

"You cannot deny, ladies, that in this case the man's love was the greater of the two; nevertheless, it was so well requited that I would gladly have all lovers equally rewarded."

"Then," said Hircan, "there would be more manifest fools among men and women than ever there were."

"Do you call it folly," said Oisille, "to love virtuously in youth and then to turn this love wholly to God?"

"If melancholy and despair be praiseworthy," answered Hircan, laughing, "I will acknowledge that Pauline and her lover are well worthy of praise."

"True it is," said Geburon, "that God has many ways of drawing us to Himself, and though they seem evil in the beginning, yet in the end they are good."

"Moreover," said Parlamente, "I believe that no man can ever love God perfectly that has not perfectly loved one of His creatures in this world."

"What do you mean by loving perfectly?" asked Saffredent. "Do you consider that those frigid beings who worship their mistresses in silence and from afar are perfect lovers?"

"I call perfect lovers," replied Parlamente, "those who seek perfection of some kind in the objects of their love, whether beauty, or goodness, or grace, ever tending to virtue, and who have such noble and upright hearts that they would rather die than do base things, contrary and repugnant to honour and conscience. For the soul, which was created for nothing but to return to its sovereign good, is, whilst enclosed in the body, ever desirous of attaining to it. But since the senses, through which the soul receives knowledge, are become dim and carnal through the sin of our first parent, they can show us only those visible things that approach towards perfection; and these the soul pursues, thinking to find in outward beauty, in a visible grace and in the moral virtues, the supreme, absolute beauty, grace and virtue. But when it has sought and tried these external things and has failed to find among them that which it really loves, the soul passes on to others; wherein it is like a child, which, when very young, will be fond of dolls and other trifles, the prettiest its eyes can see, and will heap pebbles together in the idea that these form wealth; but as the child grows older he becomes fond of living dolls, and gathers together the riches that are needful for earthly life. And when he learns by greater experience that in all these earthly things there is neither perfection nor happiness, he is fain to seek Him who is the Creator and Author of happiness and perfection. Albeit, if God should not give him the eye of Faith, he will be in danger of passing from ignorance to infidel philosophy, since it is Faith alone that can teach and instil that which is right; for this, carnal and fleshly man can never comprehend." (6)

6 The whole of this mystical dissertation appears to have been inspired by some remarks in Castiglione's Libro del Cortegiano—which Margaret was no doubt well acquainted with, as it was translated into French in 1537 by Jacques Colin, her brother's secretary. This work, which indeed seems to have suggested several passages in the Heptameron, was at that time as widely read in France as in Italy and Spain.—B. J. and D.

"Do you not see," said Longarine, "that uncultivated ground which bears plants and trees in abundance, however useless they may be, is valued by men, because it is hoped that it will produce good fruit if this be sown in it? In like manner, if the heart of man has no feeling of love for visible things, it will never arrive at the love of God by the sowing of His Word, for the soul of such a heart is barren, cold and worthless."

"That," said Saffredent, "is the reason why most of the doctors are not spiritual. They never love anything but good wine and dirty, ill-favoured serving-women, without making trial of the love of honourable ladies."

"If I could speak Latin well," said Simontault, "I would quote you St. John's words: 'He that loveth not his brother whom he hath seen, how can he love God whom he hath not seen?' (7) From visible things we are led on to love those that are invisible."

"If," said Ennasuite, "there be a man as perfect as you say, *quis est ille et laudabimus eum?*" (8)

7 I St. John, iv. 20.

8 We have been unable to find this anywhere in the Scriptures.—Ed.

"There are men," said Dagoucin, "whose love is so strong and true that they would rather die than harbour a wish contrary to the honour and conscience of their mistress, and who at the same time are unwilling that she or others should know what is in their hearts."

"Such men," said Saffredent, "must be of the nature of the chameleon, which lives on air. (9) There is not a man in the world but would fain declare his love and know that it is returned; and further, I believe that love's fever is never so great, but it quickly passes off when one knows the contrary. For myself, I have seen manifest miracles of this kind."

9 A popular fallacy. The chameleon undoubtedly feeds upon small insects.—D.

"I pray you then," said Ennasuite, "take my place and tell us about some one that was recalled from death to life by having discovered in his mistress the very opposite of his desire."

"I am," said Saffredent, "so much afraid of displeasing the ladies, whose faithful servant I have always been and shall always be, that without an express command from themselves I should never have dared to speak of their imperfections. However, in obedience to them, I will hide nothing of the truth."

[The Lord de Riant finding the Widow with her Groom]

TALE XX

The Lord of Riant, being greatly in love with a widow lady and finding her the contrary of what he had desired and of what she had often declared herself to be, was so affected thereby that in a moment resentment had power to extinguish the flame which neither length of time nor lack of opportunity had been able to quench. (1)

1 The unpleasant discovery related in this tale is attributed by Margaret to a gentleman of Francis I.'s household, but a similar incident figures in the introduction to the Arabian Nights. Ariosto also tells much the same tale in canto xxviii. of his Rolando Furioso, and another version of it will be found in No. 24 of Morlini's Novella, first issued at Naples in 1520. Subsequent to the Heptameron it supplied No. 29 of the Comptes du Monde Adventureux, figured in a rare imitation of the Cent Nouvelles Nouvelles printed at Rouen early in the seventeenth century, and was introduced by La Fontaine into his well-known tale Joconde. On the other hand, there is certainly a locality called Rians in Provence, just beyond the limits of Dauphiné, and moreover among Francis I.'s "equerries of the stable" there was a Monsieur dc Rian who received a salary of 200 livres a year from 1522 to 1529.—See the roll of the officers of the King's Household in the French National Archives, Sect. Histor., K. 98. Some extracts from Brantôme bearing on the story will be found in the Appendix to this vol. (A).—L. and En.

In the land of Dauphiné there lived a gentleman named the Lord of Riant; he belonged to the household of King Francis the First, and was as handsome and worshipful a gentleman as it was possible to see. He had long been the lover of a widow lady, whom he loved and revered so exceedingly that, for fear of losing her favour, he durst not solicit of her that which he most desired. Now, since he knew himself to be a handsome man and one worthy to be loved, he fully believed what she often swore to him—namely, that she loved him more than any living man, and that if she were led to do aught for any gentleman, it would be for him alone, who was the most perfect she had ever known. She at the same time begged him to rest satisfied with this virtuous love and to seek nothing further, and assured him that if she found him unreasonably aiming at more, he would lose her altogether. The poor gentleman was not only satisfied, but he deemed himself very fortunate in having gained the heart of a lady who appeared to him so full of virtue.

It would take too long to tell you his love-speeches, his lengthened visits to her, and the journeys he took in order to see her; it is enough to say that this poor martyr, consumed by so pleasing a fire that the more one burns the more one wishes to burn, continually sought for the means of increasing his martyrdom.

One day the fancy took him to go post-haste to see the lady whom he loved better than himself, and whom he prized beyond every other woman in the world. On reaching her house, he inquired where she was, and was told that she had just come from vespers, and was gone into the warren to finish her devotions there. He dismounted from his horse and went straight to the warren where she was to be found, and here he met with some of her women, who told him that she had gone to walk alone in a large avenue.

He was more than ever beginning to hope that some good fortune awaited him, and continued searching for her as carefully and as quietly as he could, desiring above all things to find her alone. He came in this way to a summer-house formed of bended boughs, the fairest and pleasantest place imaginable, (2) and impatient to see the object of his love, he went in; and there beheld the lady lying on the grass in the arms of a groom in her service, who was as ill-favoured, foul and disreputable as the Lord of Riant was handsome, virtuous and gentle.

2 For a description of a summer-house of the kind referred to, see Cap's edition of Palissy's Dessein du Jardin Délectable, p. 69. Palissy there describes some summer-houses formed of young elmtrees, with seats, columns, friezes, and a roofing so cunningly contrived of bent boughs that the rain could not penetrate into the interior. It is to some such construction that Queen Margaret refers.—M.

I will not try to depict to you his resentment, but it was so great that in a moment it had power to extinguish the flame which neither length of time nor lack of opportunity had been able to impair.

"Madam," he said to her, being now as full of indignation as once he had been of love, "much good may this do you! (3) The revelation of your wickedness has to-day cured me, and freed me from the continual anguish that was caused by the virtue I believed to be in you." (4)

3 The French words here are "prou face," which in Margaret's time were very generally used in lieu of "Amen" or "So be it."—M.

4 In Joconde La Fontaine gives the end of the adventure as follows:—
"Sans rencontrer personne et sans etre entendu
Il monte dans sa chambre et voit près de la dame
Un lourdaud de valet sur son sein étendu.
Tous deux dormaient. Dans cet abord Joconde
Voulut les envoyer dormir en l'autre monde,
Mais cependant il n'en fit rien
Et mon avis est qu'il fit bien."

Both in La Fontaine's Conte and in Ariosto's Rolando the lady is the Queen, and the favoured lover the King's dwarf. —Ed.

And with this farewell he went back again more quickly than he had come.

The unhappy woman made him no other reply than to put her hand to her face; for being unable to hide her shame, she covered her eyes that she might not see him who in spite of her deceit now perceived it only too clearly.

"And so, ladies, if you are not minded to love perfectly, do not, I pray you, seek to deceive and annoy an honest man for vanity's sake; for hypocrites are rewarded as they deserve, and God favours those who love with frankness."

"Truly," said Oisille, "you have kept us a proper tale for the end of the day. But that we have all sworn to speak the truth, I could not believe that a woman of that lady's condition could be so wicked both in soul and in body, and leave so gallant a gentleman for so vile a muleteer."

"Ah, madam," said Hircan, "if you knew what a difference there is between a gentleman who has worn armour and been at the wars all his life, and a well-fed knave that has never stirred from home, you would excuse the poor widow."

"I do not believe," said Oisille, "whatever you may say, that you could admit any possible excuse for her."

"I have heard," said Simontault, "that there are women who like to have apostles to preach of their virtue and chastity, and treat them as kindly and familiarly as possible, saying that but for the restraints of honour and conscience they would grant them their desire. And so these poor fools, when speaking in company of their mistresses, swear that they would thrust their fingers into the fire without fear of burning in proof that these ladies are virtuous women, since they have themselves thoroughly tested their love. Thus are praised by honourable men, those who show their true nature to such as are like themselves; and they choose such as would not have courage to speak, or, if they did, would not be believed by reason of their low and degraded position."

"That," said Longarine, "is an opinion which I have before now heard expressed by jealous and suspicious men, but it may indeed be called painting a chimera. And even although it be true of one wretched woman, the same suspicion cannot attach to all."

"Well," said Parlamente, "the longer we talk in this way, the longer will these good gentlemen play the critics over Simontault's tale, and all at our own expense. So in my opinion we had better go to vespers, and not cause so much delay as we did yesterday."

The company agreed to this proposal, and as they were going Oisille said:—

"If any one gives God thanks for having told the truth to-day, Saffredent ought to implore His forgiveness for having raked up so vile a story against the ladies."

"By my word," replied Saffredent, "what I told you was true, albeit I only had it upon hearsay. But were I to tell you all that I have myself seen of women, you would have need to make even more signs of the cross than the priests do in consecrating a church."

"Repentance is a long way off," said Geburon, "when confession only increases the sin."

"Since you have so bad an opinion of women," said Parlamente, "they ought to deprive you of their honourable society and friendship."

"There are some women," he returned, "who have acted towards me so much in accordance with your advice, in keeping me far away from things that are honourable and just, that could I do and say worse to them, I should not neglect doing so, in order that I might stir them up to revenge me on her who does me so much wrong."

Whilst he spoke these words, Parlamente put on her mask (5) and went with the others into the church, where they found that although the bell had rung for vespers, there was not a single monk, present to say them.

5 Little masks hiding only the upper part of the face, and called tourets-de-nez, were then frequently worn by ladies of rank. Some verses by Christine de Pisan show them to have been in vogue already in the fourteenth century. In the MS. copy of Margaret's poem of La Coche presented to the Duchess of Etampes, the ladies in the different miniatures are frequently shown wearing masks of the kind referred to. Some curious particulars concerning these tourets will be found in M. Léon do Laborde's Le Palais Mazarin et les grandes habitations de ville et de campagne au XVIIe Siècle, Paris, 1846, 8vo, p. 314.—L.

The monks, indeed, had heard that the company assembled in the meadow to tell the pleasantest tales imaginable, and being fonder of pleasure than of their prayers, they had gone and hidden themselves in a ditch, where they lay flat on their bellies behind a very thick hedge; and they had there listened so eagerly to the stories that they had not heard the ringing of the monastery bell, as was soon clearly shown, for they returned in such great haste that they almost lacked breath to begin the saying of vespers.

After the service, when they were asked why they had been so late and had chanted so badly, they confessed that they had been to listen to the tales; whereupon, since they were so desirous of hearing them, it was granted that they might sit and listen at their ease every day behind the hedge.

Supper-time was spent joyously in discoursing of such matters as they had not brought to an end in the meadow. And this lasted through the evening, until Oisille begged them to retire so that their minds might be the more alert on the morrow, after a long, sound sleep, one hour of which before midnight was, said she, better than three after it. Accordingly the company parted one from another, betaking themselves to their respective rooms; and in this wise ended the Second Day.

THIRD DAY

On the Third Day are recounted Tales of the Ladies who have only sought what was honourable in Love, and of the hypocrisy and wickedness of the Monks.

PROLOGUE

Though it was yet early when the company entered the hall on the morrow, they found Madame Oisille there before them. She had been meditating for more than half-an-hour upon the lesson that she was going to read; and if she had contented them on the first and second days, she assuredly did no less on the third; indeed, but that one of the monks came in search of them they would not have heard high mass, for so intent were they upon listening to her that they did not even hear the bell.

When they had piously heard mass, and had dined with temperance to the end that the meats might in no sort hinder the memory of each from acquitting itself as well as might be when their several turns came, they withdrew to their apartments, there to consult their note-books until the wonted hour for repairing to the meadow was come. When it had arrived they were not slow to make the pleasant excursion, and those who were prepared to tell of some merry circumstance already showed mirthful faces that gave promise of much laughter. When they were seated, they asked Saffredent to whom he would give his vote for the beginning of the Third Day.

"I think," said he, "that since my offence yesterday was as you say very great, and I have knowledge of no story that might atone for it, I ought to give my vote to Parlamente, who, with her sound understanding, will be able to praise the ladies sufficiently to make you forget such truth as you heard from me."

"I will not undertake," said Parlamente, "to atone for your offences, but I will promise not to imitate them. Wherefore, holding to the truth that we have promised and vowed to utter, I propose to show you that there are ladies who in their loves have aimed at nought but virtue. And since she of whom I am going to speak to you came of an honourable line, I will just change the names in my story but nothing more; and I pray you, ladies, believe that love has no power to change a chaste and virtuous heart, as you will see by the tale I will now begin to tell."

[Rolandine Conversing With Her Husband]

TALE XXI

Having remained unmarried until she was thirty years of age, Rolandine, recognising her father's neglect and her mistress's disfavour, fell so deeply in love with a bastard gentleman that she promised him marriage; and this being told to her father he treated her with all the harshness imaginable, in order to make her consent to the dissolving of the marriage; but she continued steadfast in her love until she had received certain tidings of the Bastard's death, when she was wedded to a gentleman who bore the same name and arms as did her own family.

There was in France a Queen (1) who brought up in her household several maidens belonging to good and noble houses. Among others there was one called Rolandine, (2) who was near akin to the Queen; but the latter, being for some reason unfriendly with the maiden's father, showed her no great kindness.

Now, although this maiden was not one of the fairest—nor yet indeed was she of the ugliest—she was nevertheless so discreet and virtuous that many persons of great consequence sought her in marriage. They had, however, but a cold reply; for the father (3) was so fond of his money that he gave no thought to his daughter's welfare, while her mistress, as I have said, bore her but little favour, so that she was sought by none who desired to be advanced in the Queen's good graces.

1 This is evidently Anne of Brittany, elder daughter of Duke Francis II. and wife in turn of Charles VIII. and Louis XII. Brantôme says: "She was the first to form that great Court of ladies which we have seen since her time until now; she always had a very great suite of ladies and maids, and never refused fresh ones; far from it, indeed, for she would inquire of the noblemen at Court if they had daughters, and would ask that they might be sent to her."—Lalanne's OEuvres de Brantôme, vol. vii. p. 314—L.

2 This by the consent of all the commentators is Anne de Rohan, elder daughter of John II. Viscount de Rohan, Count of Porhoët, Léon and La Garnache, by Mary of Brittany, daughter of Duke Francis I. The date of Anne de Rohan's birth is not exactly known, but she is said to have been about thirty years of age at the time of the tale, though the incidents related extend over a somewhat lengthy period. However, we know that Anne was ultimately married to Peter de Rohan in 1517, when, according to her marriage contract, she was over thirty-six years old (Les Preuves de Histoire ecclésiastique et civile de Bretagne, 1756, vol. v. col. 940). From this we may assume that she was thirty in or about 1510. The historical incidents alluded to in the tale would, however, appear to have occurred (as will be shown by subsequent notes) between 1507 and 1509, and we are of opinion that the Queen of Navarre has made her heroine rather older than she really was, and that the story indeed begins in or about 1505, when Rolandine can have been little more than five or six and twenty.—Ed.

3 See notes to Tale XL. (vol. iv).

Thus, owing to her father's neglect and her mistress's disdain, the poor maiden continued unmarried for a long while; and this at last made her sad at heart, not so much because she longed to be married as because she was ashamed at not being so, wherefore she forsook the vanities and pomps of the Court and gave herself up wholly to the worship of God. Her sole delight consisted in prayer or needlework, and thus in retirement she passed her youthful years, living in the most virtuous and holy manner imaginable.

Now, when she was approaching her thirtieth year, there was at Court a gentleman who was a Bastard of a high and noble house; (4) he was one of the pleasantest comrades and most worshipful men of his day, but he was wholly without fortune, and possessed of such scant comeliness that no lady would have chosen him for her lover.

4 One cannot absolutely identify this personage; but judging by what is said of him in the story—that he came of a great house, that he was very brave but poor, neither rich enough to marry Rolandine nor handsome enough to be made a lover of, and that a lady, who was a near relative of his, came to the Court after his intrigue had been going on for a couple of years—he would certainly appear to be John, Bastard of Angoulôme, a natural son of Count John the Good, and consequently half-brother to Charles of Angoulôme (who married Louise of Savoy) and uncle to Francis I. and Queen Margaret. In Père Anselme's Histoire Généalogique de la Maison de France, vol. i. p. 210 B. there is a record of the letters of legitimisation granted to the Bastard of Angoulême at his father's request in June 1458, and M. Paul Lacroix points out that if Rolandine's secret marriage to him took place in or about 1508, he would then have been about fifty years old, hardly the age for a lover. The Bastard is, however, alluded to in the tale as a man of mature years, and as at the outset of the intrigue (1505) he would have been but forty-seven, we incline with M. de Lincy to the belief that he is the hero of it.—Eu.

Thus this poor gentleman had continued unmated, and as one unfortunate often seeks out another, he addressed himself to Rolandine, whose fortune, temper and condition were like his own. And while they were engaged in mutually lamenting their woes, they became very fond of each other, and finding that they were companions in misfortune, sought out one another everywhere, so that they might exchange consolation, in this wise setting on foot a deep and lasting attachment.

Those who had known Rolandine so very retiring that she would speak to none, were now greatly shocked on seeing her unceasingly with the well-born Bastard, and told her governess that she ought not to suffer their long talks together. The governess, therefore, remonstrated with Rolandine, and told her that every one was shocked at her conversing so freely with a man who was neither rich enough to marry her nor handsome enough to be her lover.

To this Rolandine, who had always been rebuked rather for austereness than for worldliness, replied—

"Alas, mother, you know that I cannot have a husband of my own condition, and that I have always shunned such as are handsome and young, fearing to fall into the same difficulties as others. And since this gentleman is discreet and virtuous, as you yourself know, and tells me nothing that is not honourable and right, what harm can I have done to you and to those that have spoken of the matter, by seeking from him some consolation in my grief?"

The poor old woman, who loved her mistress more than she loved herself, replied—

"I can see, my lady, that you speak the truth, and know that you are not treated by your father and mistress as you deserve to be. Nevertheless, since people are speaking about your honour in this way, you ought to converse with him no longer, even were he your own brother."

"Mother," said Rolandine, "if such be your counsel I will observe it; but 'tis a strange thing to be wholly without consolation in the world."

The Bastard came to talk with her according to his wont, but she told him everything that her governess had said to her, and, shedding tears, besought him to have no converse with her for a while, until the rumour should be past and gone; and to this he consented at her request.

Being thus cut off from all consolation, they both began, however, to feel such torment during their separation as neither had ever known before. For her part she did not cease praying to God, journeying and fasting; for love, heretofore unknown to her, caused her such exceeding disquiet as not to leave her an hour's repose. The well-born Bastard was no better off; but, as he had already resolved in his heart to love her and try to wed her, and had thought not only of his love but of the honour that it would bring him if he succeeded in his design, he reflected that he must devise a means of making his love known to her and, above all, of winning the governess to his side. This last he did by protesting to her the wretchedness of her poor mistress, who was being robbed of all consolation. At this the old woman, with many tears, thanked him for the honourable affection that he bore her mistress, and they took counsel together how he might speak with her. They planned that Rolandine should often feign to suffer from headache, to which noise is exceedingly distressful; so that, when her companions went into the Queen's apartment, she and the Bastard might remain alone, and in this way hold converse together.

The Bastard was overjoyed at this, and, guiding himself wholly by the governess's advice, had speech with his sweetheart whensoever he would. However, this contentment lasted no great while, for the Queen, who had but little love for Rolandine, inquired what she did so constantly in her room. Some one replied that it was on account of sickness, but another, who possessed too good a memory for the absent, declared that the pleasure she took in speaking with the Bastard must needs cause her headache to pass away.

The Queen, who deemed the venial sins of others to be mortal ones in Rolandine, sent for her and forbade her ever to speak to the Bastard except it were in the royal chamber or hall. The maiden gave no sign, but replied—

"Had I known, madam, that he or any one beside were displeasing to you, I should never have spoken to him."

Nevertheless she secretly cast about to find some other plan of which the Queen should know nothing, and in this she was successful. On Wednesdays, Fridays and Saturdays she was wont to fast, and would then stay with her governess in her own room, where, while the others were at supper, she was free to speak with the man whom she was beginning to love so dearly.

The more they were compelled to shorten their discourse, the more lovingly did they talk; for they stole the time even as a robber steals something that is of great worth. But, in spite of all their secrecy, a serving-man saw the Bastard go into the room one fast day, and reported the matter in a quarter where it was not concealed from the Queen. The latter was so wroth that the Bastard durst enter the ladies' room no more. Yet, that he might not lose the delight of converse with his love, he often made a pretence of going on a journey, and returned in the evening to the church or chapel of the castle (5) dressed as a Grey Friar or a Jacobin, or disguised so well in some other way that none could know him; and thither, attended by her governess, Rolandine would go to have speech with him.

5 This would be either the château of Amboise or that of Blois, we are inclined to think the latter, as Louis XII. more frequently resided there.—Ed.

Then, seeing how great was the love she bore him, he feared not to say—

"You see, fair lady, what risk I run in your service, and how the Queen has forbidden you to speak with me. You see, further, what manner of man is your father, who has no thought whatsoever of bestowing you in marriage. He has rejected so many excellent suitors, that I know of none, whether near or far, that can win you. I know that I am poor, and that you could not wed a gentleman that were not richer than I; yet, if love and good-will were counted wealth, I should hold myself for the richest man on earth. God has given you great wealth, and you are like to have even more. Were I so fortunate as to be chosen for your husband, I would be your husband, lover and servant all my life long; whereas, if you take one of equal consideration with yourself—and such a one it were hard to find—he will seek to be the master, and will have more regard for your wealth than for your person, and for the beauty of others than for your virtue; and, whilst enjoying the use of your wealth, he will fail to treat you, yourself, as you deserve. And now my longing to have this delight, and my fear that you will have none such with another, impel me to pray that you will make me a happy man, and yourself the most contented and best treated wife that ever lived."

When Rolandine heard the very words that she herself had purposed speaking to him, she replied with a glad countenance—

"I am well pleased that you have been the first to speak such words as I had a long while past resolved to say to you. For the two years that I have known you I have never ceased to turn over in my mind all the arguments for you and against you that I was able to devise; but now that I am at last resolved to enter into the married state, it is time that 1 should make a beginning and choose some one with whom I may look to dwell with tranquil mind. And I have been able to find none, whether handsome, rich, or nobly born, with whom my heart and soul could agree excepting yourself alone. I know that in marrying you I shall not offend God, but rather do what He enjoins, while as to his lordship my father, he has regarded my welfare so little, and has rejected so many offers, that the law suffers me to marry without fear of being disinherited; though, even if I had only that which is now mine, I should, in marrying such a husband as you, account myself the richest woman in the world. As to the Queen, my mistress, I need have no qualms in displeasing her in order to obey God, for never had she any in hindering me from any blessing that I might have had in my youth. But, to show you that the love I bear you is founded upon virtue and honour, you must promise that if I agree to this marriage, you will not seek its consummation until my father be dead, or until I have found a means to win his consent."

To this the Bastard readily agreed, whereupon they exchanged rings in token of marriage, and kissed each other in the church in the presence of God, calling upon Him to witness their promise; and never afterwards was there any other familiarity between them save kissing only.

This slender delight gave great content to the hearts of these two perfect lovers; and, secure in their mutual affection, they lived for some time without seeing each other. There was scarcely any place where honour might be won to which the Bastard did not go, rejoicing that he could not now continue a poor man, seeing that God had bestowed on him a rich wife; and she during his absence steadfastly cherished their perfect love, and made no account of any other living man. And although there were some who asked her in marriage, the only answer they had of her was that, since she had remained unwedded for so long a time, she desired to continue so for ever. (6)

6 The speeches of Rolandine and the Bastard should be compared with some of Clement Marot's elegies, notably with one in which he complains of having been surprised while conversing with his mistress in a church.—B. J.

This reply came to the ears of so many people, that the Queen heard of it and asked her why she spoke in that way. Rolandine replied that it was done in obedience to herself, who had never been pleased to marry her to any man who would have well and comfortably provided for her; accordingly, being taught by years and patience to be content with her present condition, she would always return a like answer whensoever any one spoke to her of marriage.

When the wars were over, (7) and the Bastard had returned to Court, she never spoke to him in presence of others, but always repaired to some church and there had speech with him under pretence of going to confession; for the Queen had forbidden them both, under penalty of death, to speak together except in public. But virtuous love, which recks naught of such a ban, was more ready to find them means of speech than were their enemies to spy them out; the Bastard disguised himself in the habit of every monkish order he could think of, and thus their virtuous intercourse continued, until the King repaired to a pleasure house he had near Tours. (8)

7 The wars here referred to would be one or another of Louis XII.'s Italian expeditions, probably that of 1507, when the battle of Aignadel was fought.—Ed.

8 This would no doubt be the famous château of Plessis-lez-Tours, within a mile of Tours, and long the favourite residence of Louis XI. Louis XII. is known to have sojourned at Plessis in 1507, at the time when the States-general conferred upon him the title of "Father of the People." English tourists often visit Plessis now adays in memory of Scott's "Quentin Durward," but only a few shapeless ruins of the old structure are left.—M. and Ed.

This, however, was not near enough for the ladies to go on foot to any other church but that of the castle, which was built in such a fashion that it contained no place of concealment in which the confessor would not have been plainly recognised.

But if one opportunity failed them, love found them another and an easier one, for there came to the Court a lady to whom the Bastard was near akin. This lady was lodged, together with her son, (9) in the King's abode; and the young Prince's room projected from the rest of the King's apartments in such a way that from his window it was possible to see and to speak to Rolandine, for his window and hers were just at the angle made by the two wings of the house.

9 This lady would be Louise of Savoy. She first came to the Court at Amboise in 1499, a circumstance which has led some commentators to place the incidents of this story at that date. But she was at Blois on various occasions between 1507 and 1509, to negotiate and attend the marriage of her daughter Margaret with the Duke of Alençon. Louis XII. having gone from Blois to Plessis in 1507, Louise of Savoy may well have followed him thither. Her son was, of course, the young Duke de Valois, afterwards Francis I.—Ed.

In this room of hers, which was over the King's presence-chamber, all the noble damsels that were Rolandine's companions were lodged with her. She, having many times observed the young Prince at his window, made this known to the Bastard through her governess; and he, having made careful observation of the place, feigned to take great pleasure in reading a book about the Knights of the Round Table (10) which was in the Prince's room.

10 Romances of chivalry were much sought after at this time. Not merely were there MS. copies of these adorned with miniatures, but we find that L'Histoire du Saint Gréai, La Vie et les Prophéties de Merlin, and Les Merveilleux Faits et Gestes du Noble Chevalier Lancelot du Lac were printed in France in the early years of the sixteenth century.—B.J.

And when every one was going to dinner, he would beg a valet to let him finish his reading, shut up in the room, over which he promised to keep good guard. The servants knew him to be a kinsman of his master and one to be trusted, let him read as much as he would. Rolandine, on her part, would then come to her window; and, so that she might be able to make a long stay at it, she pretended to have an infirmity in the leg, and accordingly dined and supped so early that she no longer frequented the ladies' table. She likewise set herself to work a coverlet of crimson silk, (11) and fastened it at the window, where she desired to be alone; and, when she saw that none was by, she would converse with her husband, who contrived to speak in such a voice as could not be overheard; and whenever any one was coming, she would cough and make a sign, so that the Bastard might withdraw in good time.

11 In the French, "Ung lût de reseul:" reticella—i.e., a kind of open work embroidery very fashionable in those days, and the most famous designers of which were Frederic Vinciolo, Dominic de Sara, and John Cousin the painter. Various sixteenth and seventeenth century books on needlework, still extant, give some curious information concerning this form of embroidery.—M.

Those who kept watch upon them felt sure that their love was past, for she never stirred from the room in which, as they thought, he could assuredly never see her, since it was forbidden him to enter it.

One day, however, the young Prince's mother, (12) being in her son's room, placed herself at the window where this big book lay, and had not long been there when one of Rolandine's companions, who was at the window in the opposite room, greeted her and spoke to her. The lady asked her how Rolandine did; whereon the other replied that she might see her if she would, and brought her to the window in her nightcap. Then, when they had spoken together about her sickness, they withdrew from the window on either side.

12 Louise of Savoy.

The lady, observing the big book about the Round Table, said to the servant who had it in his keeping—

"I am surprised that young folk can waste their time in reading such foolishness."

The servant replied that he marvelled even more that people accounted sensible and of mature age should have a still greater liking for it than the young; and he told her, as matter for wonderment, how her cousin the Bastard would spend four or five hours each day in reading this fine book. Straightway there came into the lady's mind the reason why he acted thus, and she charged the servant to hide himself somewhere, and take account of what the Bastard might do. This the man did, and found that the Bastard's book was the window to which Rolandine came to speak with him, and he, moreover, heard many a love-speech which they had thought to keep wholly secret.

On the morrow he related this to his mistress, who sent for the Bastard, and after chiding him forbade him to return to that place again; and in the evening she spoke of the matter to Rolandine, and threatened, if she persisted in this foolish love, to make all these practices known to the Queen.

Rolandine, whom nothing could dismay, vowed that in spite of all that folks might say she had never spoken to him since her mistress had forbidden her to do so, as might be learned both from her companions and from her servants and attendants. And as for the window, she declared that she had never spoken at it to the Bastard. He, however, fearing that the matter had been discovered, withdrew out of harm's way, and was a long time without returning to Court, though not without writing to Rolandine, and this in so cunning a manner that, in spite of the Queen's vigilance, never a week went by but she twice heard from him.

When he no longer found it possible to employ monks as messengers, as he had done at first, he would send a little page, dressed now in one colour and now in another; and the page used to stand at the doorways through which the ladies were wont to pass, and deliver his letters secretly in the throng. But one day, when the Queen was going out into the country, it chanced that one who was charged to look after this matter recognised the page, and hastened after him; but he, being keen-witted and suspecting that he was being pursued, entered the house of a poor woman who was boiling her pot on the fire, and there forthwith burned his letters. The gentleman who followed him stripped him naked and searched through all his clothes; but he could find nothing, and so let him go. And the boy being gone, the old woman asked the gentleman why he had so searched him.

"To find some letters," he replied, "which I thought he had upon him."

"You could by no means have found them," said the old woman, "they were too well hidden for that."

"I pray you," said the gentleman, in the hope of getting them before long, "tell me where they were."

However, when he heard that they had been thrown into the fire, he perceived that the page had proved more crafty than himself, and forthwith made report of the matter to the Queen.

From that time, however, the Bastard no longer employed the page or any other child, but sent an old servant of his, who, laying aside all fear of the death which, as he well knew, was threatened by the Queen against all such as should interfere in this matter, undertook to carry his master's letters to Rolandine. And having come to the castle where she was, he posted himself on the watch at the foot of a broad staircase, beside a doorway through which all the ladies were wont to pass. But a serving-man, who had aforetime seen him, knew him again immediately and reported the matter to the Queen's Master of the Household, who quickly came to arrest him. However, the discreet and wary servant, seeing that he was being watched from a distance, turned towards the wall as though he desired to make water, and tearing the letter he had into the smallest possible pieces, threw them behind a door. Immediately afterwards he was taken and thoroughly searched, and nothing being found on him, they asked him on his oath whether he had not brought letters, using all manner of threats and persuasions to make him confess the truth; but neither by promises nor threats could they draw anything from him.

Report of this having been made to the Queen, some one in the company bethought him that it would be well to look behind the door near which the man had been taken. This was done, and they found what they sought, namely the pieces of the letter. Then the King's confessor was sent for, and he, having put the pieces together on a table, read the whole of the letter, in which the truth of the marriage, that had been so carefully concealed, was made manifest; for the Bastard called Rolandine nothing but "wife." The Queen, who was in no mind, as she should have been, to hide her neighbour's transgressions, made a great ado about the matter, and commanded that all means should be employed to make the poor man confess the truth of the letter. And indeed, when they showed it to him, he could not deny it; but for all they could say or show, he would say no more than at first. Those who had him in charge thereupon brought him to the brink of the river, and put him into a sack, declaring that he had lied to God and to the Queen, contrary to proven truth. But he was minded to die rather than accuse his master, and asked for a confessor; and when he had eased his conscience as well as might be, he said to them—

"Good sirs, I pray you tell the Bastard, my master, that I commend the lives of my wife and children to him, for right willingly do I yield up my own in his service. You may do with me what you will, for never shall you draw from me a word against my master."

Thereupon, all the more to affright him, they threw him in the sack into the water, calling to him—

"If you will tell the truth, you shall be saved."

Finding, however, that he answered nothing, they drew him out again, and made report of his constancy to the Queen, who on hearing of it declared that neither the King nor herself were so fortunate in their followers as was this gentleman the Bastard, though he lacked even the means to requite them. She then did all that she could to draw the servant into her own service, but he would by no means consent to forsake his master. However, by the latter's leave, he at last entered the Queen's service, in which he lived in happiness and contentment.

The Queen, having learnt the truth of the marriage from the Bastard's letter, sent for Rolandine, whom with a wrathful countenance she several times called "wretch" instead of "cousin," reproaching her with the shame that she had brought both upon her father's house and her mistress by thus marrying without her leave or commandment.

Rolandine, who had long known what little love her mistress bore her, gave her but little in return. Moreover, since there was no love between them, neither was there fear; and as Rolandine perceived that this reprimand, given her in presence of several persons, was prompted less by affection than by a desire to put her to shame, and that the Queen felt more pleasure in chiding her than grief at finding her in fault, she replied with a countenance as glad and tranquil as the Queen's was disturbed and wrathful—

"If, madam, you did not know your own heart, such as it is, I would set forth to you the ill-will that you have long borne my father (13) and myself; but you do, indeed, know this, and will not deem it strange that all the world should have an inkling of it too. For my own part, madam, I have perceived it to my dear cost, for had you been pleased to favour me equally as you favour those who are not so near to you as myself, I were now married to your honour as well as to my own; but you passed me over as one wholly a stranger to your favour, and so all the good matches I might have made passed away before my eyes, through my father's neglect and the slenderness of your regard. By reason of this treatment I fell into such deep despair, that, had my health been strong enough in any sort to endure a nun's condition, I would have willingly entered upon it to escape from the continual griefs your harshness brought me.

13 Of all those with pretensions to the Duchy of Brittany, the Viscount de Rohan had doubtless the best claim, though he met with the least satisfaction. It was, however, this reason that led the Queen [Anne of Brittany] to treat him with such little regard. It was with mingled grief and resentment that this proud princess realised how real were the Viscount's rights; moreover, she never forgave him for having taken up arms against her in favour of France; and seeking an opportunity to avenge herself, she found one in giving the Viscount but little satisfaction in the matter of his pretensions."—Dora Morice's Histoire ecclésiastique et civile de Bretagne, Paris, 1756, vol. ii. p. 231.—L.

"Whilst in this despair I was sought by one whose lineage would be as good as my own if mutual love were rated as high as a marriage ring; for you know that his father would walk before mine. He has long wooed and loved me; but you, madam, who have never forgiven me the smallest fault nor praised me for any good deed, you—although you knew from experience that I was not wont to speak of love or worldly things, and that I led a more retired and religious life than any other of your maids—forthwith deemed it strange that I should speak with a gentleman who is as unfortunate in this life as I am myself, and one, moreover, in whose friendship I thought and looked to have nothing save comfort to my soul. When I found myself wholly baffled in this design, I fell into great despair, and resolved to seek my peace as earnestly as you longed to rob me of it; whereupon we exchanged words of marriage, and confirmed them with promise and ring. Wherefore, madam, methinks you do me a grievous wrong in calling me wicked, seeing that in this great and perfect love, wherein opportunity, had I so desired, would not have been lacking, no greater familiarity has passed between us than a kiss. I have waited in the hope that, before the consummation of the marriage, I might by the grace of God win my father's heart to consent to it. I have given no offence to God or to my conscience, for I have waited till the age of thirty to see what you and my father would do for me, and have kept my youth in such chastity and virtue that no living man can bring up aught against me. But when I found that I was old and without hope of being wedded suitably to my birth and condition, I used the reason that God has given me, and resolved to marry a gentleman after my own heart. And this I did not to gratify the lust of the eye, for you know that he is not handsome; nor the lust of the flesh, for there has been no carnal consummation of our marriage; nor the ambition and pride of life, for he is poor and of small rank; but I took account purely and simply of the worth that is in him, for which every one is constrained to praise him, and also of the great love that he bears me, and that gives me hope of having a life of quietness and kindness with him. Having carefully weighed all the good and the evil that may come of it, I have done what seems to me best, and, after considering the matter in my heart for two years, I am resolved to pass the remainder of my days with him. And so firm is my resolve that no torment that may be inflicted upon me, nor even death itself, shall ever cause me to depart from it. Wherefore, madam, I pray you excuse that which is indeed very excusable, as you yourself must realise, and suffer me to dwell in that peace which I hope to find with him."

The Queen, finding her so steadfast of countenance and so true of speech, could make no reply in reason, but continued wrathfully rebuking and reviling her, bursting into tears and saying—

"Wretch that you are! instead of humbling yourself before me, and repenting of so grievous a fault, you speak hardily with never a tear in your eye, and thus clearly show the obstinacy and hardness of your heart. But if the King and your father give heed to me, they will put you into a place where you will be compelled to speak after a different fashion."

"Madam," replied Rolandine, "since you charge me with speaking too hardily, I will e'en be silent if you give me not permission to reply to you."

Then, being commanded to speak, she went on—

"'Tis not for me, madam, to speak to you, my mistress and the greatest Princess in Christendom, hardily and without the reverence that I owe to you, nor have I purposed doing so; but I have no defender to speak for me except the truth, and as this is known to me alone, I am forced to utter it fearlessly in the hope that, when you know it, you will not hold me for such as you have been pleased to name me. I fear not that any living being should learn how I have comported myself in the matter that is laid to my charge, for I know that I have offended neither against God nor against my honour. And this it is that enables me to speak without fear; for I feel sure that He who sees my heart is on my side, and with such a Judge in my favour, I were wrong to fear such as are subject to His decision. Why should I weep? My conscience and my heart do not at all rebuke me, and so far am I from repenting of this matter, that, were it to be done over again, I should do just the same. But you, madam, have good cause to weep both for the deep wrong that you have done me throughout my youth, and for that which you are now doing me, in rebuking me publicly for a fault that should be laid at your door rather than at mine. Had I offended God, the King, yourself, my kinsfolk or my conscience, I were indeed obstinate and perverse if I did not greatly repent with tears; but I may not weep for that which is excellent, just and holy, and which would have received only commendation had you not made it known before the proper time. In doing this, you have shown that you had a greater desire to compass my dishonour than to preserve the honour of your house and kin. But, since such is your pleasure, madam, I have nothing to say against it; command me what suffering you will, and I, innocent though I am, will be as glad to endure as you to inflict it. Wherefore, madam, you may charge my father to inflict whatsoever torment you would have me undergo, for I well know that he will not fail to obey you. It is pleasant to know that, to work me ill, he will wholly fall in with your desire, and that as he has neglected my welfare in submission to your will, so will he be quick to obey you to my hurt. But I have a Father in Heaven, and He will, I am sure, give me patience equal to all the evils that I foresee you preparing for me, and in Him alone do I put my perfect trust."

The Queen, beside herself with wrath, commanded that Rolandine should be taken from her sight and put into a room alone, where she might have speech with no one. However, her governess was not taken from her, and through her Rolandine acquainted the Bastard with all that had befallen her, and asked him what he would have her do. He, thinking that his services to the King might avail him something, came with all speed to the Court. Finding the King at the chase, he told him the whole truth, entreating him to favour a poor gentleman so far as to appease the Queen and bring about the consummation of the marriage.

The King made no reply except to ask—

"Do you assure me that you have wedded her?"

"Yes, sire," said the Bastard, "but by word of mouth alone; however, if it please you, we'll make an ending of it."

The King bent his head, and, without saying anything more, returned straight towards the castle, and when he was nigh to it summoned the Captain of his Guard, and charged him to take the Bastard prisoner.

However, a friend who knew and could interpret the King's visage, warned the Bastard to withdraw and betake himself to a house of his that was hard by, saying that if the King, as he expected, sought for him, he should know of it forthwith, so that he might fly the kingdom; whilst if, on the other hand, things became smoother, he should have word to return. The Bastard followed this counsel, and made such speed that the Captain of the Guards was not able to find him.

The King and Queen took counsel together as to what they should do with the hapless lady who had the honour of being related to them, and by the Queen's advice it was decided that she should be sent back to her father, and that he should be made acquainted with the whole truth.

But before sending her away they caused many priests and councillors to speak with her and show her that, since her marriage consisted in words only, it might by mutual agreement readily be made void; and this, they urged, the King desired her to do in order to maintain the honour of the house to which she belonged.

She made answer that she was ready to obey the King in all such things as were not contrary to her conscience, but that those whom God had brought together man could not put asunder. She therefore begged them not to tempt her to anything so unreasonable; for if love and goodwill founded on the fear of God were the true and certain marriage ties, she was linked by bonds that neither steel nor flame nor water could sever. Death alone might do this, and to death alone would she resign her ring and her oath. She therefore prayed them to gainsay her no more; for so strong of purpose was she that she would rather keep faith and die than break it and live.

This steadfast reply was repeated to the King by those whom he had appointed to speak with her, and when it was found that she could by no means be brought to renounce her husband, she was sent to her father, and this in so pitiful a plight that all who beheld her pass wept to see her. And although she had done wrong, her punishment was so grievous and her constancy so great, that her wrongdoing was made to appear a virtue.

When her father heard the pitiful tale, he would not see her, but sent her away to a castle in a forest, which he had aforetime built for a reason well worthy to be related. (14) There he kept her in prison for a long time, causing her to be told that if she would give up her husband he would treat her as his daughter and set her free.

14 The famous château of Josselin in Morbihan. See notes to Tale XL., vol. lv.—Ed.

Nevertheless she continued firm, for she preferred the bonds of prison together with those of marriage, to all the freedom in the world without her husband. And, judging from her countenance, all her woes seemed but pleasant pastimes to her, since she was enduring them for one she loved.

And now, what shall I say of men? The Bastard, who was so deeply beholden to her, as you have seen, fled to Germany where he had many friends, and there showed by his fickleness that he had sought Rolandine less from true and perfect love than from avarice and ambition; for he fell deeply in love with a German lady, and forgot to write to the woman who for his sake was enduring so much tribulation. However cruel Fortune might be towards them, they were always able to write to each other, until he conceived this foolish and wicked love. And Rolandine's heart gaining an inkling of it, she could no longer rest.

And afterwards, when she found that his letters were colder and different from what they had been before, she suspected that some new love was separating her from her husband, and doing that which all the torments and afflictions laid upon herself had been unable to effect. Nevertheless, her perfect love would not pass judgment on mere suspicion, so she found a means of secretly sending a trusty servant, not to carry letters or messages to him, but to watch him and discover the truth. When this servant had returned from his journey, he told her that the Bastard was indeed deeply in love with a German lady, and that according to common report he was seeking to marry her, for she was very rich.

These tidings brought extreme and unendurable grief to Rolandine's heart, so that she fell grievously sick. Those who knew the cause of her sickness, told her on behalf of her father that, with this great wickedness on the part of the Bastard before her eyes, she might now justly renounce him. They did all they could to persuade her to that intent, but, notwithstanding her exceeding anguish, she could not be brought to change her purpose, and in this last temptation again gave proof of her great love and surpassing virtue. For as love grew less and less on his part, so did it grow greater on hers, and in this way make good that which was lost. And when she knew that the entire and perfect love that once had been shared by both remained but in her heart alone, she resolved to preserve it there until one or the other of them should die. And the Divine Goodness, which is perfect charity and true love, took pity upon her grief and long suffering, in such wise that a few days afterwards the Bastard died while occupied in seeking after another woman. Being advised of this by certain persons who had seen him laid in the ground, she sent to her father and begged that he would be pleased to speak with her.

Her father, who had never spoken to her since her imprisonment, came without delay. He listened to all the pleas that she had to urge, and then, instead of rebuking her or killing her as he had often threatened, he took her in his arms and wept exceedingly.

"My daughter," he said, "you are more in the right than I, for if there has been any wrongdoing in this matter, I have been its principal cause. But now, since God has so ordered it, I would gladly atone for the past."

He took her home and treated her as his eldest daughter. A gentleman who bore the same name and arms as did her own family sought her in marriage; he was very sensible and virtuous, (15) and he thought so much of Rolandine, whom he often visited, that he gave praise to what others blamed in her, perceiving that virtue had been her only aim. The marriage, being acceptable both to Rolandine and to her father, was concluded without delay.

It is true, however, that a brother she had, the sole heir of their house, would not grant her a portion, for he charged her with having disobeyed her father. And after his father's death he treated her so harshly that she and her husband (who was a younger son) had much ado to live. (16)

15 Peter de Rohan-Gié, Lord of Frontenay, third son of Peter de Rohan, Lord of Gié, Marshal of Prance and preceptor to Francis I. As previously stated, the marriage took place in 1517, and eight years later the husband was killed at Pavia.—Ed.

16 Anne de Rohan (Rolandine) had two brothers, James and Claud. Both died without issue. Some particulars concerning them will be found in the notes to Tale XL. The father's death, according to Anselme, took place in 1516, that is, prior to Anne's marriage.—Ed.

However, God provided for them, for the brother that sought to keep everything died suddenly one day, leaving behind him both her wealth, which he was keeping back, and his own.

Thus did she inherit a large and rich estate, whereon she lived piously and virtuously and in her husband's love. And after she had brought up the two sons that God gave to them, (17) she yielded with gladness her soul to Him in whom she had at all times put her perfect trust.

17 Anne's sons were René and Claud. Miss Mary Robinson (The Fortunate Lovers, London, 1887) believes René to be "Saffredent," and his wife Isabel d'Albret, sister of Queen Margaret's husband Henry of Navarre, to be "Nomerfide."—Ed.

"Now, ladies, let the men who would make us out so fickle come forward and point to an instance of as good a husband as this lady was a good wife, and of one having like faith and steadfastness. I am sure they would find it so difficult to do this, that I will release them from the task rather than put them to such exceeding toil. But as for you, ladies, I would pray you, for the sake of maintaining your own fair fame, either to love not at all, or else to love as perfectly as she did. And let none among you say that this lady offended against her honour, seeing that her constancy has served to heighten our own."

"In good sooth, Parlamente," said Oisille, "you have indeed told us the story of a woman possessed of a noble and honourable heart; but her constancy derives half its lustre from the faithlessness of a husband that could leave her for another."

"I think," said Longarine, "that the grief so caused must have been the hardest to bear. There is none so heavy that the love of two united lovers cannot support it; but when one fails in his duty, and leaves the whole of the burden to the other, the load becomes too heavy to be endured."

"Then you ought to pity us," said Geburon, "for we have to bear the whole burden of love, and you will not put out the tip of a finger to relieve us."

"Ah, Geburon," said Parlamente, "the burdens of men and of women are often different enough. The love of a woman, being founded on godliness and honour, is just and reasonable, and any man that is false to it must be reckoned a coward, and a sinner against God and man. On the other hand, most men love only with reference to pleasure, and women, being ignorant of their ill intent, are sometimes ensnared; but when God shows them how vile is the heart of the man whom they deemed good, they may well draw back to save their honour and reputation, for soonest ended is best mended."

"Nay, that is a whimsical idea of yours," said Hircan, "to hold that an honourable woman may in all honour betray the love of a man; but that a man may not do as much towards a woman. You would make out that the heart of the one differs from that of the other; but for my part, in spite of their differences in countenance and dress, I hold them to be alike in inclination, except indeed that the guilt which is best concealed is the worst."

Thereto Parlamente replied with some heat—

"I am well aware that in your opinion the best women are those whose guilt is known."

"Let us leave this discourse," said Simontault; "for whether we take the heart of man or the heart of woman, the better of the twain is worth nothing. And now let us see to whom Parlamente is going to give her vote, so that we may hear some fine tale."

"I give it," she said, "to Geburon."

"Since I began," (18) he replied, "by talking about the Grey friars, I must not forget those of Saint Benedict, nor an adventure in which they were concerned in my own time. Nevertheless, in telling you the story of a wicked monk, I do not wish to hinder you from having a good opinion of such as are virtuous; but since the Psalmist says 'all men are liars,' and in another place, 'there is none that doeth good, no not one,' (19) I think we are bound to look upon men as they really are. If there be any virtue in them, we must attribute it to Him who is its source, and not to the creature. Most people deceive themselves by giving overmuch praise or glory to the latter, or by thinking that there is something good in themselves. That you may not deem it impossible for exceeding lust to exist under exceeding austerity, listen to what befel in the days of King Francis the First."

18 See the first tale he tells, No. 5, vol. i.—Ed.

19 Psalms cxvi. 11 and xiv. 3.

[Sister Marie and the Prior]

TALE XXII

Sister Marie Heroet, being unchastely solicited by a Prior of Saint-Martin-in-the-Fields, was by the grace of God enabled to overcome his great temptations, to the Prior's exceeding confusion and her own glory. (1)

1 This story is historical, and though M. Frank indicates points of similarity between it and No. xxvii. of St. Denis' Comptes du Monde Adventureux, and No. vi. of Masuccio de Solerac's Novellino, these are of little account when one remembers that the works in question were written posterior to the Heptameron. The incidents related in the tale must have occurred between 1530 and 1535. The Abbey of Saint-Martin-in-the-Fields stood on the site of the present Conservatoire des Arts et Métiers, Paris.—Ed.

In the city of Paris there was a Prior of Saint-Martin-in-the-Fields, whose name I will keep secret for the sake of the friendship I bore him. Until he reached the age of fifty years, his life was so austere that the fame of his holiness was spread throughout the entire kingdom, and there was not a prince or princess but showed him high honour when he came to visit them. There was further no monkish reform that was not wrought by his hand, so that people called him the "father of true monasticism." (2)

He was chosen visitor to the illustrious order of the "Ladies of Fontevrault," (3) by whom he was held in such awe that, when he visited any of their convents, the nuns shook with very fear, and to soften his harshness towards them would treat him as though he had been the King himself in person. At first he would not have them do this, but at last, when he was nearly fifty-five years old, he began to find the treatment he had formerly contemned very pleasant; and reckoning himself the mainstay of all monasticism, he gave more care to the preservation of his health than had heretofore been his wont. Although the rules of his order forbade him ever to partake of flesh, he granted himself a dispensation (which was more than he ever did for another), declaring that the whole burden of conventual affairs rested upon him; for which reason he feasted himself so well that, from being a very lean monk he became a very fat one.

2 This prior was Stephen Gentil, who succeeded Philip Bourgoin on December 15, 1508, and died November 6, 1536. The Gallia Christiana states that in 1524 he reformed an abbey of the diocese of Soissons, but makes no mention of his appointment as visitor to the abbey of Fontevrault. Various particulars concerning him will be found in Manor's Monasterii Regalis S. Martini de Campis, &c. Parisiis, 1636, and in Gallia Christiana, vol. vii. col. 539.—L.

3 The abbey of Fontevrault, near Saumur, Maine-et-Loire, was founded in 1100 by Robert d'Arbrissel, and comprised two conventual establishments, one for men and the other for women. Prior to his death, d'Arbrissel abdicated his authority in favour of Petronilla de Chemillé, and from her time forward monks and nuns alike were always under the sway of an abbess—this being the only instance of the kind in the history of the Roman Catholic Church. Fourteen of the abbesses were princesses, and several of these were of the blood royal of France. In the abbey church were buried our Henry II., Eleanor of Guienne, Richard Coeur-de-Lion, and Isabella of Angoulême; their tombs are still shown, though the abbey has become a prison, and its church a refectory.—Ed.

Together with this change of life there was wrought also a great change of heart, so that he now began to cast glances upon countenances which aforetime he had looked at only as a duty; and, contemplating charms which were rendered even more desirable by the veil, he began to hanker after them. Then, to satisfy this longing, he sought out such cunning devices that at last from being a shepherd he became a wolf, so that in many a convent, where there chanced to be a simple maiden, he failed not to beguile her. But after he had continued this evil life for a long time, the Divine Goodness took compassion upon the poor, wandering sheep, and would no longer suffer this villain's triumph to endure, as you shall hear.

One day he went to visit the convent of Gif, (4) not far from Paris, and while he was confessing all the nuns, it happened that there was one among them called Marie Heroet, whose speech was so gentle and pleasing that it gave promise of a countenance and heart to match.

4 Gif, an abbey of the Benedictine order, was situated at five leagues from Paris, in the valley of Chevreuse, on the bank of the little river Yvette. A few ruins of it still remain. It appears to have been founded in the eleventh century.—See Le Beuf s Histoire du Diocèse de Paris, vol. viii. part viii. p. 106, and Gallia Christiana, vol. vii. col. 596.—L. and D.

The mere sound of her voice moved him with a passion exceeding any that he had ever felt for other nuns, and, while speaking to her, he bent low to look at her, and perceiving her rosy, winsome mouth, could not refrain from lifting her veil to see whether her eyes were in keeping therewith. He found that they were, and his heart was filled with so ardent a passion that, although he sought to conceal it, his countenance became changed, and he could no longer eat or drink. When he returned to his priory, he could find no rest, but passed his days and nights in deep disquiet, seeking to devise a means whereby he might accomplish his desire, and make of this nun what he had already made of many others. But this, he feared, would be difficult, seeing that he had found her to be prudent of speech and shrewd of understanding; moreover, he knew himself to be old and ugly, and therefore resolved not to employ words but to seek to win her by fear.

Accordingly, not long afterwards, he returned to the convent of Gif aforesaid, where he showed more austerity than he had ever done before, and spoke wrathfully to all the nuns, telling one that her veil was not low enough, another that she carried her head too high, and another that she did not do him reverence as a nun should do. So harsh was he in respect of all these trifles, that they feared him as though he had been a god sitting on the throne of judgment.

Being gouty, he grew very weary in visiting all the usual parts of the convent, and it thus came to pass that about the hour for vespers, an hour which he had himself fixed upon, he found himself in the dormitory, when the Abbess said to him—

"Reverend father, it is time to go to vespers."

"Go, mother," he replied, "do you go to vespers. I am so weary that I will remain here, yet not to rest but to speak to Sister Marie, of whom I have had a very bad report, for I am told that she prates like a worldly-minded woman."

The Abbess, who was aunt to the maiden's mother, begged him to reprove her soundly, and left her alone with him and a young monk who accompanied him.

When he found himself alone with Sister Marie, he began to lift up her veil, and to tell her to look at him. She answered that the rule of her order forbade her to look at men.

"It is well said, my daughter," he replied, "but you must not consider us monks as men."

Then Sister Marie, fearing to sin by disobedience, looked him in the face; but he was so ugly that she though it rather a penance than a sin to look at him.

The good father, after telling her at length of his goodwill towards her, sought to lay his hand upon her breasts; but she repulsed him, as was her duty; whereupon, in great wrath, he said to her—

"Should a nun know that she has breasts?"

"I know that I have," she replied, "and certes neither you nor any other shall ever touch them. I am not so young and ignorant that I do not know the difference between what is sin and what is not."

When he saw that such talk would not prevail upon her, he adopted a different plan, and said—

"Alas, my daughter, I must make known to you my extreme need. I have an infirmity which all the physicians hold to be incurable unless I have pleasure with some woman whom I greatly love. For my part, I would rather die than commit a mortal sin; but, when it comes to that, I know that simple fornication is in no wise to be compared with the sin of homicide. So, if you love my life, you will preserve it for me, as well as your own conscience from cruelty."

She asked him what manner of pleasure he desired to have. He replied that she might safely surrender her conscience to his own, and that he would do nothing that could be a burden to either.

Then, to let her see the beginning of the pastime that he sought, he took her in his arms and tried to throw her upon a bed. She, recognising his evil purpose, defended herself so well with arms and voice that he could only touch her garments. Then, when he saw that all his devices and efforts were being brought to naught, he behaved like a madman and one devoid not only of conscience but of natural reason, for, thrusting his hand under her dress, he scratched wherever his nails could reach with such fury that the poor girl shrieked out, and fell swooning at full length upon the floor.

Hearing this cry, the Abbess came into the dormitory; for while at vespers she had remembered that she had left her niece's daughter alone with the good father, and feeling some scruples of conscience, she had left the chapel and repaired to the door of the dormitory in order to learn what was going on. On hearing her niece's voice, she pushed open the door, which was being held by the young monk.

And when the Prior saw the Abbess coming, he pointed to her niece as she lay in a swoon, and said—

"Assuredly, mother, you are greatly to blame that you did not inform me of Sister Marie's condition. Knowing nothing of her weakness, I caused her to stand before me, and, while I was reproving her, she swooned away as you see."

They revived her with vinegar and other remedies, and found that she had wounded her head in her fall. When she was recovered, the Prior, fearing that she would tell her aunt the reason of her indisposition, took her aside and said to her—

"I charge you, my daughter, if you would be obedient and hope for salvation, never to speak of what I said to you just now. You must know that it was my exceeding love for you that constrained me, but since I see that you do not wish to love me, I will never speak of it to you again. However, if you be willing, I promise to have you chosen Abbess of one of the three best convents in the kingdom."

She replied that she would rather die in perpetual imprisonment than have any lover save Him who had died for her on the cross, for she would rather suffer with Him all the evils the world could inflict than possess without Him all its blessings. And she added that he must never again speak to her in such a manner, or she would inform the Abbess; whereas, if he kept silence, so would she.

Thereupon this evil shepherd left her, and in order to make himself appear quite other than he was, and to again have the pleasure of looking upon her he loved, he turned to the Abbess and said—

"I beg, mother, that you will cause all your nuns to sing a *Salve Regina* in honour of that virgin in whom I rest my hope."

While this was being done, the old fox did nothing but shed tears, not of devotion, but of grief at his lack of success. All the nuns, thinking that it was for love of the Virgin Mary, held him for a holy man, but Sister Marie, who knew his wickedness, prayed in her heart that one having so little reverence for virginity might be brought to confusion.

And so this hypocrite departed to St. Martin's, where the evil fire that was in his heart did not cease burning night and day alike, prompting him to all manner of devices in order to compass his ends. As he above all things feared the Abbess, who was a virtuous woman, he hit upon a plan to withdraw her from the convent, and betook himself to Madame de Vendôme, who was at that time living at La Fère, where she had founded and built a convent of the Benedictine order called Mount Olivet. (5)

5 This is Mary of Luxemburg, Countess of St. Paul-de-Conversan, Marie and Soissons, who married, first, James of

Savoy, and secondly, Francis de Bourbon, Count of Vendôme. The latter, who accompanied Charles VIII. to Italy, was killed at Vercelli in October 1495, when but twenty-five years old. His widow did not marry again, but retired to her château of La Fère near Laon (Aisne), where late in 1518 she founded a convent of Benedictine nuns, which, according to the Gallia Christiana, she called the convent of Mount Calvary. This must be the establishment alluded to by Queen Margaret, who by mistake has called it Mount Olivet, i.e., the Mount of Olives. Madame de Vendôme died at a very advanced age on April 1, 1546.—See Anselme's Histoire Généalogique, vol. i. p. 326.—L.

Speaking in the quality of a prince of reformers, he gave her to understand that the Abbess of the aforesaid Mount Olivet lacked the capacity to govern such a community. The worthy lady begged him to give her another that should be worthy of the office, and he, who asked nothing better, counselled her to have the Abbess of Gif, as being the most capable in France. Madame de Vendôme sent for her forthwith, and set her over the convent of Mount Olivet.

As the Prior of St. Martin's had every monastic vote at his disposal, he caused one who was devoted to him to be chosen Abbess of Gif, and this being accomplished, he went to Gif to try once more whether he might win Sister Marie Heroet by prayers or honied words. Finding that he could not succeed, he returned in despair to his priory of St. Martin's, and in order to achieve his purpose, to revenge himself on her who was so cruel to him, and further to prevent the affair from becoming known, he caused the relics of the aforesaid convent of Gif to be secretly stolen at night, and accusing the confessor of the convent, a virtuous and very aged man, of having stolen them, he cast him into prison at St. Martin's.

Whilst he held him captive there, he stirred up two witnesses who in ignorance signed what the Prior commanded them, which was a statement that they had seen the confessor in a garden with Sister Marie, engaged in a foul and wicked act; and this the Prior sought to make the old monk confess. But he, who knew all the Prior's misdoings, entreated him to bring him before the Chapter, saying that there, in presence of all the monks, he would tell the truth of all that he knew. The Prior, fearing that the confessor's justification would be his own condemnation, would in no wise grant this request; and, finding him firm of purpose, he treated him so ill in prison that some say he brought about his death, and others that he forced him to lay aside his robe and betake himself out of the kingdom of France. Be that as it may, the confessor was never seen again.

The Prior, thinking that he had now a sure hold upon Sister Marie, repaired to the convent, where the Abbess, chosen for this purpose, gainsaid him in nothing. There he began to exercise his authority as visitor, and caused all the nuns to come one after the other into a room that he might hear them, as is the fashion at a visitation. When the turn of Sister Marie, who had now lost her good aunt, had come, he began speaking to her in this wise—

"Sister Marie, you know of what crime you are accused, and that your pretence of chastity has availed you nothing, since you are well known to be the very contrary of chaste."

"Bring here my accuser," replied Sister Marie, with steadfast countenance, "and you will see whether in my presence he will abide by his evil declaration."

"No further proof is needed," he said, "since the confessor has been found guilty."

"I hold him for too honourable a man," said Sister Marie, "to have confessed so great a lie; but even should he have done so, bring him here before me, and I will prove the contrary of what he says."

The Prior, finding that he could in no wise move her, thereupon said—

"I am your father, and seek to save your honour. For this reason I will leave the truth of the matter to your own conscience, and will believe whatever it bids you say. I ask you and conjure you on pain of mortal sin to tell me truly whether you were indeed a virgin when you were placed in this house?"

"My father," she replied, "I was then but five years old, and that age must in itself testify to my virginity."

"Well, my daughter," said the Prior, "have you not since that time lost this flower?"

She swore that she had kept it, and that she had had no hindrance in doing so except from himself. Whereto he replied that he could not believe it, and that the matter required proof.

"What proof," she asked, "would you have?"

"The same as from the others," said the Prior; "for as I am visitor of souls, even so am I visitor of bodies also. Your abbesses and prioresses have all passed through my hands, and you need have no fear if I visit your virginity. Wherefore throw yourself upon the bed, and lift the forepart of your garments over your face."

"You have told me so much of your wicked love for me," Sister Marie replied in wrath, "that I think you seek rather to rob me of my virginity than to visit it. So understand that I shall never consent."

Thereupon he said to her that she was excommunicated for refusing him the obedience which Holy Church commanded, and that, if she did not consent, he would dishonour her before the whole Chapter by declaring the evil that he knew of between herself and the confessor.

But with fearless countenance she replied—

"He that knows the hearts of His servants shall give me as much honour in His presence as you can give me shame in the presence of men; and since your wickedness goes so far, I would rather it wreaked its cruelty upon me than its evil passion; for I know that God is a just judge."

Then the Prior departed and assembled the whole Chapter, and, causing Sister Marie to appear on her knees before him, he said to her with wondrous malignity—

"Sister Marie, it grieves me to see that the good counsels I have given you have been of no effect, and to find you fallen into such evil ways that, contrary to my wont, I must needs lay a penance upon you. I have examined your confessor concerning certain crimes with which he is charged, and he has confessed to me that he has abused your person in the place where the witnesses say that they saw him. And so I command that, whereas I had formerly raised you to honourable rank as Mistress of the Novices, you shall now be the lowest placed of all, and further, shall eat only bread and water on the ground, and in presence of all the Sisters, until you have shown sufficient penitence to receive forgiveness."

Sister Marie had been warned by one of her companions, who was acquainted with the whole matter, that if she made any reply displeasing to the Prior, he would put her *in pace*—that is, in perpetual imprisonment—and she therefore submitted to this sentence, raising her eyes to heaven, and praying Him who had enabled her to withstand sin, to grant her patience for the endurance of tribulation. The Prior of St. Martin's further commanded that for the space of three years she should neither speak with her mother or kinsfolk when they came to see her, nor send any letters save such as were written in community.

The miscreant then went away and returned no more, and for a long time the unhappy maiden continued in the tribulation that I have described.

But her mother, who loved her best of all her children, was much astonished at receiving no tidings from her; and told one of her sons, who was a prudent and honourable gentleman, (6) that she thought her daughter was dead, and that the nuns were hiding it from her in order that they might receive the yearly payment. She, therefore, begged him to devise some means of seeing his sister.

6 It is conjectured by M. Lacroix that this "prudent and honourable gentleman," Mary Heroet's brother, was Antoine Heroet or Hérouet, alias La Maisonneuve, who at one time was a valet and secretary to Queen Margaret, and so advanced himself in life that he died Bishop of Digne in 1544. He was the author of La Parfaite Amie, L'Androgyne, and De n'aimer point sans être aimé, poems of a semi-metaphysical, semi-amorous character such as might have come from Margaret's own pen. Whether he was Mary Heroet's brother or not, it is at least probable that he was her relative.-B. J. and L.

He went forthwith to the convent, where he met with the wonted excuses, being told that for three years his sister had not stirred from her bed. But this did not satisfy him, and he swore that, if he did not see her, he would climb over the walls and force his way into the convent. Thereupon, being in great fear, they brought his sister to him at the grating, though the Abbess stood so near that she could not tell her brother aught that was not heard. But she had prudently set down in writing all that I have told you, together with a thousand others of the Prior's devices to deceive her, which 'twould take too long to relate.

Yet I must not omit to mention that at the time when her aunt was Abbess, the Prior, thinking that his ugliness was the cause of her refusal, had caused Sister Marie to be tempted by a handsome young monk, in the hope that if she yielded to this man through love, he himself might afterwards obtain her through fear. The young monk aforesaid spoke to her in a garden with gestures too shameful to be mentioned, whereat the poor maiden ran to the Abbess, who was talking with the Prior, and cried out—

"Mother, they are not monks, but devils, who visit us here!"

Thereupon the Prior, in great fear of discovery, began to laugh, and said—

"Assuredly, mother, Sister Marie is right."

Then, taking Sister Marie by the hand, he said to her in presence of the Abbess—

"I had heard that Sister Marie spoke very well, and so constantly that she was deemed to be worldly-minded. For this reason I constrained myself, contrary to my natural inclination, to speak to her in the way that worldly men speak to women—at least in books, for in point of experience I am as ignorant as I was on the day when I was born. Thinking, however, that only my years and ugliness led her to discourse in so virtuous a fashion, I commanded my young monk to speak to her as I myself had done, and, as you see, she has virtuously resisted him. So highly, therefore, do I think of her prudence and virtue, that henceforward she shall rank next after you and shall be Mistress of the Novices, to the intent that her excellent disposition may ever increase in virtue."

This act, with many others, was done by this worthy monk during the three years that he was in love with the nun. She, however, as I have said, gave her brother in writing, through the grating, the whole story of her pitiful fortunes; and this her brother brought to her mother, who came, overwhelmed with despair, to Paris. Here she found the Queen of Navarre, only sister to the King, and showing her the piteous story, said—

"Madam, trust no more in these hypocrites. I thought that I had placed my daughter within the precincts of Paradise, or on the high road thither, whereas I have placed her in the precincts of Hell, and in the hands of the vilest devils imaginable. The devils, indeed, do not tempt us unless temptation be our pleasure, but these men will take by force when they cannot win by love."

The Queen of Navarre was in great concern, for she trusted wholly in the Prior of St. Martin's, to whose care she had committed her sisters-inlaw, the Abbesses of Montivilliers and Caen. (7) On the other hand, the enormity of the crime so horrified her and made her so desirous of avenging the innocence of this unhappy maiden, that she communicated the matter to the King's Chancellor, who happened also to be Legate in France. (8)

7 The abbess of Montivilliers was Catherine d'Albret, daughter of John d'Albret, King of Navarre and sister of Queen Margaret's husband, Henry. At first a nun at the abbey of St. Magdalen at Orleans, she became twenty-eighth abbess of Montivilliers near Havre. She was still living in 1536. (Gallia Christ., vol. xi. col. 285). The abbess of Caen was Magdalen d'Albret, Catherine's sister. She took the veil at Fontevrault in 1527, subsequently became thirty-third abbess of the Trinity at Caen, and died in November 1532. (Gallia Christ., vol. xi. col. 436).—L.

8 This is the famous Antony Duprat, Francis I.'s favourite minister. Born in 1463, he became Chancellor in 1515, and his wife dying soon afterwards, he took orders, with the result that he was made Archbishop of Sens and Cardinal. It was in 1530 that he was appointed Papal Legate in France, so that the incidents related in this tale cannot have occurred at an earlier date. Duprat died in July 1535, of grief, it is said, because Francis I. would not support him in his ambitious scheme to secure possession of the papal see, as successor to Clement VII.-B. J. and Ed.

The Prior was sent for, but could find nothing to plead except that he was seventy years of age, and addressing himself to the Queen of Navarre he begged that, for all the good she had ever wished to do him, and in token of all the services he had rendered or had desired to render her, she would be pleased to bring these proceedings to a close, and he would acknowledge that Sister Marie was a pearl of honour and chastity.

On hearing this, the Queen of Navarre was so astonished that she could make no reply, but went off and left him there. The unhappy man then withdrew in great confusion to his monastery, where he would suffer none to see him, and where he lived only one year afterwards. And Sister Marie Heroet, now reputed as highly as she deserved to be, by reason of the virtues that God had given her, was withdrawn from the convent of Gif, where she had endured so much evil, and was by the King made Abbess of the the convent of Giy (9) near Montargis.

9 Giy-les-Nonains, a little village on the river Ouanne, at two leagues and a half from Montargis, department of the Loiret.—L.

This convent she reformed, and there she lived like one filled with the Spirit of God, whom all her life long she ever praised for having of His good grace restored to her both honour and repose.

"There, ladies, you have a story which clearly proves the words of the Gospel, that 'God hath chosen the weak things of the world to confound the things which are mighty, and things which are despised of men hath God chosen to bring to nought the glory of those who think themselves something but are in truth nothing.' (10) And remember, ladies, that without the grace of God there is no good at all in man, just as there is no temptation that with His assistance may not be overcome. This is shown by the abasement of the man who was accounted just, and the exaltation of her whom men were willing to deem a wicked sinner. Thus are verified Our Lord's words, 'Whosoever exalteth himself shall be abased; and he that humbleth himself shall be exalted.'" (11)

10 I Corinthians i. 27, 28, slightly modified.

11 St. Luke xiv. 11 and xviii. 14.

"Alas," said Oisille, "how many virtuous persons did that Prior deceive! For I saw people put more trust in him than even in God."

"*I* should not have done so," said Nomerfide, "for such is my horror of monks that I could not confess to one. I believe they are worse than all other men, and never frequent a house without leaving disgrace or dissension behind them."

"There are good ones among them," said Oisille, "and they ought not to be judged by the bad alone; but the best are those that least often visit laymen's houses and women."

"You are right," said Ennasuite. "The less they are seen, the less they are known, and therefore the more highly are they esteemed; for companionship with them shows what they really are."

"Let us say no more about them," said Nomerfide, "and see to whom Geburon will give his vote."

"I shall give it," said he, "to Madame Oisille, that she may tell us something to the credit of Holy Church." (12)

12 In lieu of this phrase, the De Thou MS. of the Heptameron gives the following: "To make amends for his fault, if fault there were in laying bare the wretched and abominable life of a wicked Churchman, so as to put others on their guard against the hypocrisy of those resembling him, Geburon, who held Madame Oysille in high esteem, as one should hold a lady of discretion, who was no less reluctant to speak evil than prompt to praise and publish the worth which she knew to exist in others, gave her his vote, begging her to tell something to the honour of our holy religion."—L.

"We have sworn," said Oisille, "to speak the truth, and I cannot therefore undertake such a task. Moreover, in telling your tale you have reminded me of a very pitiful story which I feel constrained to relate, seeing that I am not far from the place where, in my own time, the thing came to pass. I shall tell it also, ladies, to the end that the hypocrisy of those who account themselves more religious than their neighbours, may not so beguile your understanding as to turn your faith out of the right path, and lead you to hope for salvation from any other than Him who has chosen to stand alone in the work of our creation and redemption. He is all powerful to save us unto life eternal, and, in this temporal life, to comfort us and deliver us from all our tribulations. And knowing that Satan often transforms himself into an angel of light so that the outward eye, blinded by the semblance of holiness and devotion, cannot apprehend that from which we ought to flee, I think it well to tell you this tale, which came to pass in our own time."

[The Grey Friar deceiving the Gentleman Of Périgord]

TALE XXIII

The excessive reverence shown by a gentleman of Périgord to the Order of St. Francis, brought about the miserable death of his wife, his little child and himself. (1)

1 *Etienne introduces this tale into his Apologie pour Hérodote, ch. xxi.—B. J.*

In the county of Périgord dwelt a gentleman whose devotion to St. Francis was such that in his eyes all who wore the saint's robe must needs be as holy as the saint himself. To do honour to the latter, he had caused rooms and closets to be furnished in his house for the lodgment of the brethren, and he regulated all his affairs by their advice, even to the most trifling household matters, believing that he must needs pursue the right path if he followed their good counsels.

Now it happened that this gentleman's wife, who was a beautiful woman and as discreet as she was virtuous, was brought to bed of a fine boy, whereat the love which her husband bore her was increased twofold. One day, in order to entertain his dear, he sent for one of his brothers-in-law, and just as the hour for supper was drawing nigh, there arrived also a Grey Friar, whose name I will keep secret out of regard for his Order. The gentleman was well pleased to see his spiritual father, from whom he had no secrets, and after much talk among his wife, his brother-in-law and the monk, they sat down to supper. While they were at table the gentleman cast his eyes upon his wife, who was indeed beautiful and graceful enough to be desired of a husband, and thereupon asked this question aloud of the worthy father—

"Is it true, father, that a man commits mortal sin if he lies with his wife at the time of her lying-in?" (2)

2 *Meaning the period between her delivery and her churching.—Ed.*

The worthy father, whose speech and countenance belied his heart, answered with an angry look—

"Undoubtedly, sir, I hold this to be one of the very greatest sins that can be committed in the married state. The blessed Virgin Mary would not enter the temple until the days of her purification were accomplished, although she had no need of these; and if she, in order to obey the law, refrained from going to the temple wherein was all her consolation, you should of a surety not fail to abstain from such slight pleasure. Moreover, physicians say that there is great risk to the offspring so begotten."

When the gentleman heard these words, he was greatly downcast, for he had hoped that the good Friar would give him the permission he sought; however, he said no more. Meanwhile the worthy father, who had drunk more than was needful, looked at the lady, (3) thinking to himself that, if he were her husband, he would ask no Friar's advice before lying with her; and just as a fire kindles little by little until at last it envelops the whole house, so this monk began to burn with such exceeding lust that he suddenly resolved to satisfy a desire which for three years he had carried hidden in his heart.

3 The French word here is damoiselle, by which appellation the lady is called throughout the story. Her husband, being a petty nobleman, was a damoiseau, whence the name given to his wife. The word damoiselle is frequently employed in the Heptameron, and though sometimes it merely signifies an attendant on a lady, the reference is more frequently to a woman of gentle birth, whether she be spinster, wife or widow. Only women of high nobility and of the blood royal were at that time called Madame.—Ed.

After the tables had been withdrawn, he took the gentleman by the hand, and, leading him to his wife's bedside, (4) said to him in her presence—

"It moves my pity, sir, to see the great love which exists between you and this lady, and which, added to your extreme youth, torments you so sore. I have therefore determined to tell you a secret of our sacred theology which is that, although the rule be made thus strict by reason of the abuses committed by indiscreet husbands, it does not suffer that such as are of good conscience like you should be balked of all intercourse. If then, sir, before others I have stated in all its severity the command of the law, I will now reveal to you, who are a prudent man, its mildness also. Know then, my son, that there are women and women, just as there are men and men. In the first place, my lady here must tell us whether, three weeks having gone by since her delivery, the flow of blood has quite ceased?"

4 The supper would appear to have been served in the bedroom, and the tables were taken away as soon as the repast was over. It seems to us very ridiculous when on the modern stage we see a couple of lackeys bring in a table laden with viands and carry it away again as soon as the dramatis personæ have dined or supped. Yet this was the common practice in France in Queen Margaret's time.—Ed.

The lady replied that it had.

"Then," said the Friar, "I permit you to lie with her without scruple, provided that you are willing to promise me two things."

The gentleman replied that he was willing.

"The first," said the good father, "is that you speak to no one concerning this matter, but come here in secret. The second is that you do not come until two hours after midnight, so that the good lady's digestion be not hindered."

These things the gentleman promised; and he confirmed his promise with so strong an oath that the other, knowing him to be foolish rather than false, was quite satisfied.

After much converse the good father withdrew to his chamber, giving them good-night and an abundant blessing. But, as he was going, he took the gentleman by the hand, and said to him—

"You too, sir, i' faith must come, nor keep your poor lady longer awake."

Thereupon the gentleman kissed her. "Sweetheart," said he, and the good father heard him plainly, "leave the door of your room open for me."

And so each withdrew to his own chamber.

On leaving them the Friar gave no heed to sleep or to repose, and, as soon as all the noises in the house were still, he went as softly as possible straight to the lady's chamber, at about the hour when he was wont to go to matins, and finding the door open in expectation of the master's coming, he went in, cleverly put out the light, and speedily got into bed with the lady, without speaking a single word.

The lady, believing him to be her husband, said—

"How is this, love? you have kept but poorly the promise you gave last evening to our confessor that you would not come here before two o'clock."

The Friar, who was more eager for action than for contemplation, and who, moreover, was fearful of being recognised, gave more thought to satisfying the wicked desires that had long poisoned his heart than to giving her any reply; whereat the lady wondered greatly. When the friar found the husband's hour drawing near, he rose from the lady's side and returned with all speed to his own chamber.

Then, just as the frenzy of lust had robbed him of sleep, so now the fear that always follows upon wickedness would not suffer him to rest. Accordingly, he went to the porter of the house and said to him—

"Friend, your master has charged me to go without delay and offer up prayers for him at our convent, where he is accustomed to perform his devotions. Wherefore, I pray you, give me my horse and open the door without letting any one be the wiser; for the mission is both pressing and secret."

The porter knew that obedience to the Friar was service acceptable to his master, and so he opened the door secretly and let him out.

Just at that time the gentleman awoke. Finding that it was close on the hour which the good father had appointed him for visiting his wife, he got up in his bedgown and repaired swiftly to that bed whither by God's ordinance, and without need of the license of man, it was lawful for him to go.

When his wife heard him speaking beside her, she was greatly astonished, and, not knowing what had occurred, said to him—

"Nay, sir, is it possible that, after your promise to the good father to be heedful of your own health and of mine, you not only come before the hour appointed, but even return a second time? Think on it, sir, I pray you."

On hearing this, the gentleman was so much disconcerted that he could not conceal it, and said to her—

"What do these words mean? I know of a truth that I have not lain with you for three weeks, and yet you rebuke me for coming too often. If you continue to talk in this way, you will make me think that my company is irksome to you, and will drive me, contrary to my wont and will, to seek elsewhere that pleasure which, by the law of God, I should have with you."

The lady thought that he was jesting, and replied—

"I pray you, sir, deceive not yourself in seeking to deceive me; for although you said nothing when you came, I knew very well that you were here."

Then the gentleman saw that they had both been deceived, and solemnly vowed to her that he had not been with her before; whereat the lady, weeping in dire distress, besought him to find out with all despatch who it could have been, seeing that besides themselves only his brother-in-law and the Friar slept in the house.

Impelled by suspicion of the Friar, the gentleman forthwith went in all haste to the room where he had been lodged, and found it empty; whereupon, to make yet more certain whether he had fled, he sent for the man who kept the door, and asked him whether he knew what had become of the Friar. And the man told him the whole truth.

The gentleman, being now convinced of the Friar's wickedness, returned to his wife's room, and said to her—

"Of a certainty, sweetheart, the man who lay with you and did such fine things was our Father Confessor."

The lady, who all her life long had held her honour dear, was overwhelmed with despair, and laying aside all humanity and womanly nature, besought her husband on her knees to avenge this foul wrong; whereupon the gentleman immediately mounted his horse and went in pursuit of the Friar.

The lady remained all alone in her bed, with no counsel or comfort near her but her little newborn child. She reflected upon the strange and horrible adventure that had befallen her, and, without making any excuse for her ignorance, deemed herself guilty as well as the unhappiest woman in the world. She had never learned aught of the Friars, save to have confidence in good works, and seek atonement for sins by austerity of life, fasting and discipline; she was wholly ignorant of the pardon granted by our good God through the merits of His Son, the remission of sins by His blood, the reconciliation of the Father with us through His death, and the life given to sinners by His sole goodness and mercy; and so, assailed by despair based on the enormity and magnitude of her sin, the love of her husband and the honour of her house, she thought that death would be far happier than such a life as hers. And, overcome by sorrow, she fell into such despair that she was not only turned aside from the hope which every Christian should have in God, but she forgot her own nature, and was wholly bereft of common sense.

Then, overpowered by grief, and driven by despair from all knowledge of God and herself, this frenzied, frantic woman took a cord from the bed and strangled herself with her own hands.

And worse even than this, amidst the agony of this cruel death, whilst her body was struggling against it, she set her foot upon the face of her little child, whose innocence did not avail to save it from following in death its sorrowful and suffering mother. While dying, however, the infant uttered so piercing a cry that a woman who slept in the room rose in great haste and lit the candle. Then, seeing her mistress hanging strangled by the bed-cord, and the child stifled and dead under her feet, she ran in great affright to the apartment of her mistress's brother, and brought him to see the pitiful sight.

The brother, after giving way to such grief as was natural and fitting in one who loved his sister with his whole heart, asked the serving-woman who it was that had committed this terrible crime.

She replied that she did not know; but that no one had entered the room excepting her master, and he had but lately left it. The brother then went to the gentleman's room, and not finding him there, felt sure that he had done the deed. So, mounting his horse without further inquiry, he hastened in pursuit and met with him on the road as he was returning disconsolate at not having been able to overtake the Grey Friar.

As soon as the lady's brother saw his brother-in-law, he cried out to him—

"Villain and coward, defend yourself, for I trust that God will by this sword avenge me on you this day."

The gentleman would have expostulated, but his brother-in-law's sword was pressing so close upon him that he found it of more importance to defend himself than to inquire the reason of the quarrel; whereupon each dealt the other so many wounds that they were at last compelled by weariness and loss of blood to sit down on the ground face to face.

And while they were recovering breath, the gentleman asked—

"What cause, brother, has turned our deep and unbroken friendship to such cruel strife as this?"

"Nay," replied the brother-in-law, "what cause has moved you to slay my sister, the most excellent woman that ever lived, and this in so cowardly a fashion that under pretence of sleeping with her you have hanged and strangled her with the bed-cord?"

On hearing these words the gentleman, more dead than alive, came to his brother, and putting his arms around him, said—

"Is it possible that you have found your sister in the state you say?"

The brother-in-law assured him that it was indeed so.

"I pray you, brother," the gentleman thereupon replied, "hearken to the reason why I left the house."

Forthwith he told him all about the wicked Grey Friar, whereat his brother-in-law was greatly astonished, and still more grieved that he should have unjustly attacked him.

Entreating pardon, he said to him—

"I have wronged you; forgive me."

"If you were ever wronged by me," replied the gentleman, "I have been well punished, for I am so sorely wounded that I cannot hope to recover."

Then the brother-in-law put him on horseback again as well as he might, and brought him back to the house, where on the morrow he died. And the brother-in-law confessed in presence of all the gentleman's relatives that he had been the cause of his death.

However, for the satisfaction of justice, he was advised to go and solicit pardon from King Francis, first of the name; and accordingly, after giving honourable burial to husband, wife and child, he departed on Good Friday to the Court in order to sue there for pardon, which he obtained through the good offices of Master Francis Olivier, then Chancellor of Alençon, afterwards chosen by the King, for his merits, to be Chancellor of France. (5)

5 M. de Montaiglon has vainly searched the French Archives for the letters of remission granted to the gentleman. There is no mention of them in the registers of the Trésor des Chartes. Francis Olivier, alluded to above, was one of the most famous magistrates of the sixteenth century. Son of James Olivier, First President of the Parliament of Paris and Bishop of Angers, he was born in 1493 and became successively advocate, member of the Grand Council, ambassador, Chancellor of Alençon, President of the Paris Parliament, Keeper of the Seals and Chancellor of France. This latter dignity was conferred upon him through Queen Margaret's influence in April 1545. The above tale must have been written subsequent to that date. Olivier's talents were still held in high esteem under both Henry II. and Francis II.; he died in 1590, aged 67.—(Blanchard's Éloges de tous les Présidents du Parlement, &c., Paris, 1645, in-fol. p. 185.)

Ste. Marthe, in his funeral oration on Queen Margaret, refers to Olivier in the following pompous strain: "When Brinon died Chancellor of this duchy of Alençon, Francis Olivier was set in his place, and so greatly adorned this dignity by his admirable virtues, and so increased the grandeur of the office of Chancellor, that, like one of exceeding merit on whom Divine Providence, disposing of the affairs of France, has conferred a more exalted office, he is today raised to the highest degree of honour, and, even as Atlas upholds the Heavens upon his shoulders, so he by his prudence doth uphold the entire Gallic commonwealth."—M. L. and Ed.

"I am of opinion, ladies, that after hearing this true story there is none among you but will think twice before lodging such knaves in her house, and will be persuaded that hidden poison is always the most dangerous."

"Remember," said Hircan, "that the husband was a great fool to bring such a gallant to sup with his fair and virtuous wife."

"I have known the time," said Geburon, "when in our part of the country there was not a house but had a room set apart for the good fathers; but now they are known so well that they are dreaded more than bandits."

"It seems to me," said Parlamente, "that when a woman is in bed she should never allow a priest to enter the room, unless it be to administer to her the sacraments of the Church. For my own part, when I send for them, I may indeed be deemed at the point of death."

"If every one were as strict as you are," said Ennasuite, "the poor priests would be worse than excommunicated, in being wholly shut off from the sight of women."

"Have no such fear on their account," said Saffredent; "they will never want for women."

"Why," said Simontault, "'tis the very men that have united us to our wives by the marriage tie that wickedly seek to loose it and bring about the breaking of the oath which they have themselves laid upon us."

"It is a great pity," said Oisille, "that those who administer the sacraments should thus trifle with them. They ought to be burned alive."

"You would do better to honour rather than blame them," said Saffredent, "and to flatter rather than revile them, for they are men who have it in their power to burn and dishonour others. Wherefore *'sinite eos,'* and let us see to whom Oisille will give her vote."

"I give it," said she, "to Dagoucin, for he has become so thoughtful that I think he must have made ready to tell us something good."

"Since I cannot and dare not reply as I would," said Dagoucin, "I will at least tell of a man to whom similar cruelty at first brought hurt but afterwards profit. Although Love accounts himself so strong and powerful that he will go naked, and finds it irksome, nay intolerable, to go cloaked, nevertheless, ladies, it often happens that those who, following his counsel, are over-quick in declaring themselves, find themselves the worse for it. Such was the experience of a Castilian gentleman, whose story you shall now hear."

[Elisor showing the Queen her own Image]

TALE XXIV

Elisor, having unwisely ventured to discover his love to the Queen of Castile, was by her put to the test in so cruel a fashion that he suffered sorely, yet did he reap advantage therefrom.

In the household of the King and Queen of Castile, (1) whose names shall not be mentioned, there was a gentleman of such perfection in all qualities of mind and body, that his like could not be found in all the Spains. All wondered at his merits, but still more at the strangeness of his temper, for he had never been known to love or have connection with any lady. There were very many at Court that might have set his icy nature afire, but there was not one among them whose charms had power to attract Elisor; for so this gentleman was called.

1 M. Lacroix conjectures that the sovereigns referred to are Ferdinand and Isabella, but this appears to us a baseless supposition. The conduct of the Queen in the story is in no wise in keeping with what we know of Isabella's character. Queen Margaret doubtless heard this tale during her sojourn in Spain in 1525. We have consulted many Spanish works, and notably collections of the old ballads, in the hope of being able to throw some light on the incidents related, but have been no more successful than previous commentators.—Ed.

The Queen, who was a virtuous woman but by no means free from that flame which proves all the fiercer the less it is perceived, was much astonished to find that this gentleman loved none of her ladies; and one day she asked him whether it were possible that he could indeed love as little as he seemed to do.

He replied that if she could look upon his heart as she did his face, she would not ask him such a question. Desiring to know his meaning, she pressed him so closely that he confessed he loved a lady whom he deemed the most virtuous in all Christendom. The Queen did all that she could by entreaties and commands to find out who the lady might be, but in vain; whereupon, feigning great wrath, she vowed that she would never speak to him any more if he did not tell her the name of the lady he so dearly loved. At this he was greatly disturbed, and was constrained to say that he would rather die, if need were, than name her.

Finding, however, that he would lose the Queen's presence and favour in default of telling her a thing in itself so honourable that it ought not to be taken in ill part by any one, he said to her in great fear—

"I cannot and dare not tell you, madam, but the first time you go hunting I will show her to you, and I feel sure that you will deem her the fairest and most perfect lady in the world."

This reply caused the Queen to go hunting sooner than she would otherwise have done.

Elisor, having notice of this, made ready to attend her as was his wont, and caused a large steel mirror after the fashion of a corselet to be made for him, which he placed upon his breast and covered with a cloak of black frieze, bordered with purflew and gold braid. He was mounted on a coal-black steed, well caparisoned with everything needful to the equipment of a horse, and such part of this as was metal was wholly of gold, wrought with black enamel in the Moorish style. (2)

2 Damascened.—Ed.

His hat was of black silk, and to it was fastened a rich medal on which by way of device was engraved the god of Love subdued by Force, the whole enriched with precious stones. His sword and dagger were no less handsomely and choicely ordered. In a word, he was most bravely equipped, while so skilled was his horsemanship that all who saw him left the pleasures of the chase to watch the leaps and paces of his steed.

After bringing the Queen in this fashion to the place where the nets were spread, he dismounted from his noble horse and went to assist the Queen to alight from her palfrey. And whilst she was stretching out her hands to him, he threw his cloak back from before his breast, and taking her in his arms, showed her his corselet-mirror, saying—

"I pray you, madam, look here."

Then, without waiting for her reply, he set her down gently upon the ground.

When the hunt was over, the Queen returned to the castle without speaking to Elisor, but after supper she called him to her and told him that he was the greatest liar she had ever seen; for he had promised to show her at the hunt the lady whom he loved the best, but had not done so, for which reason she was resolved to hold him in esteem no more.

Elisor, fearing that the Queen had not understood the words he had spoken to her, answered that he had indeed obeyed her, for he had shown her not merely the woman but the thing also, that he loved best in all the world.

Pretending that she did not understand him, she replied that he had not, to her knowledge, shown her a single one among her ladies.

"That is true, madam," said Elisor, "but what did I show you when I helped you off your horse?"

"Nothing," said the Queen, "except a mirror on your breast."

"And what did you see in the mirror?" said Elisor.

"I saw nothing but myself," replied the Queen.

"Then, madam," said Elisor, "I have kept faith with you and obeyed your command. There is not, nor ever will there be, another image in my heart save that which you saw upon my breast. Her alone will I love, reverence and worship, not as a woman merely, but as my very God on earth, in whose hands I place my life or my death, entreating her withal that the deep and perfect affection, which was my life whilst it remained concealed, may not prove my death now that it is discovered. And though I be not worthy that you should look on me or accept me for your lover, at least suffer me to live, as hitherto, in the happy consciousness that my heart has chosen so perfect and so worthy an object for its love, wherefrom I can have no other satisfaction than the knowledge that my love is deep and perfect, seeing that I must be content to love without hope of return. And if, now knowing this great love of mine, you should not be pleased to favour me more than heretofore, at least do not deprive me of life, which for me consists wholly in the delight of seeing you as usual. I now have from you nought but what my utmost need requires, and should I have less, you will have a servant the less, for you will lose the best and most devoted that you have ever had or could ever look to have."

The Queen—whether to show herself other than she really was, or to thoroughly try the love he bore her, or because she loved another whom she would not cast off, or because she wished to hold him in reserve to put him in the place of her actual lover should the latter give her any offence—

said to him, with a countenance that showed neither anger nor content—"Elisor, I will not feign ignorance of the potency of love, and say aught to you concerning your foolishness in aiming at so high and hard a thing as the love of me; for I know that man's heart is so little under his own control, that he cannot love or hate at will. But, since you have concealed your feelings so well, I would fain know how long it is since you first entertained them."

Elisor, gazing at her beauteous face and hearing her thus inquire concerning his sickness, hoped that she might be willing to afford him a remedy. But at the same time, observing the grave and staid expression of her countenance, he became afraid, feeling himself to be in the presence of a judge whose sentence, he suspected, would be against him. Nevertheless he swore to her that this love had taken root in his heart in the days of his earliest youth, though it was only during the past seven years that it had caused him pain,—and yet, in truth, not pain, but so pleasing a sickness that its cure would be his death.

"Since you have displayed such lengthened steadfastness," said the Queen, "I must not show more haste in believing you, than you have shown in telling me of your affection. If, therefore, it be as you say, I will so test your sincerity that I shall never afterwards be able to doubt it; and having proved your pain, I will hold you to be towards me such as you yourself swear you are; and on my knowing you to be what you say, you, for your part, shall find me to be what you desire."

Elisor begged her to test him in any way she pleased, there being nothing, he said, so difficult that it would not appear very easy to him, if he might have the honour of proving his love to her; and accordingly he begged her once more to command him as to what she would to have him do.

"Elisor," she replied, "if you love me as much as you say, I am sure that you will deem nothing hard of accomplishment if only it may bring you my favour. I therefore command you, by your desire of winning it and your fear of losing it, to depart hence to-morrow morning without seeing me again, and to repair to some place where, until this day seven years, you shall hear nothing of me nor I anything of you. You, who have had seven years' experience of this love, know that you do indeed love me; and when I have had a like experience, I too shall know and believe what your words cannot now make me either believe or understand."

When Elisor heard this cruel command, he on the one hand suspected that she desired to remove him from her presence, yet, on the other, he hoped that this proof would plead more eloquently for him than any words he could utter. He therefore submitted to her command, and said—

"For seven years I have lived hopeless, bearing in my breast a hidden flame; now, however, that this is known to you, I shall spend these other seven years in patience and trust. But, madam, while I obey your command, which robs me of all the happiness that I have heretofore had in the world, what hope will you give me that at the end of the seven years you will accept me as your faithful and devoted lover?"

"Here is a ring," said the Queen, drawing one from her finger, "which we will cut in two. I will keep one half, and you shall keep the other, (3) so that I may know you by this token, if the lapse of time should cause me to forget your face."

3 This was a common practice at the time between lovers, and even between husbands and wives. There is the familiar but doubtful story of Frances de Foix, Countess of Châteaubriant, who became Francis I.'s mistress, and who is said to have divided a ring in this manner with her husband, it being understood between them that she was not to repair to Court, or even leave her residence in Brittany, unless her husband sent her as a token the half of the ring which he had kept. Francis I., we are told, heard of this, and causing a ring of the same pattern to be made, he sent half of it to the Countess, who thereupon came to Court, imagining that it was her husband who summoned her. Whether the story be true or not, it should be mentioned that the sole authority for it is Varillas, whose errors and inventions are innumerable.—Ed.

Elisor took the ring and broke it in two, giving one half of it to the Queen, and keeping the other himself. Then, more corpse-like than those who have given up the ghost, he took his leave, and went to his lodging to give orders for his departure. In doing this he sent all his attendants to his house, and departed alone with one servingman to so solitary a spot that none of his friends or kinsfolk could obtain tidings of him during the seven years.

Of the life that he led during this time, and the grief that he endured through this banishment, nothing is recorded, but lovers cannot be ignorant of their nature. At the end of the seven years, just as the Queen was one day going to mass, a hermit with a long beard came to her, kissed her hand, and presented her with a petition. This she did not look at immediately, although it was her custom to receive in her own hands all the petitions that were presented to her, no matter how poor the petitioners might be.

When mass was half over, however, she opened the petition, and found in it the half-ring which she had given to Elisor. At this she was not less glad than astonished, and before reading the contents she instantly commanded her almoner to bring her the tall hermit who had presented her the petition.

The almoner looked for him everywhere, but could obtain no tidings of him, except that some one said that he had seen him mount a horse, but knew not what road he had taken.

Whilst she was waiting for the almoner's return, the Queen read the petition, which she found to be an epistle in verse, written in the best style imaginable; and were it not that I would have you acquainted with it, I should never have dared to translate it; for you must know, ladies, that, for grace and expression, the Castilian is beyond compare the tongue which is best fitted to set forth the passion of love. The matter of the letter was as follows:—

"Time, by his puissance stern, his sov'reign might,
Hath made me learn love's character aright;
And, bringing with him, in his gloomy train,
The speechless eloquence of bitter pain,
Hath caused the unbelieving one to know
What words of love were impotent to show.
Time made my heart, aforetime, meekly bow
Unto the mastery of love; but now
Time hath, at last, revealed love to be
Far other than it once appeared to me;
And Time the frail foundation hath made clear
Whereon I purposed, once, my love to rear—
To wit, your beauty, which but served as sheath
To hide the cruelty that lurked beneath.

Yea, Time hath shown me beauty's nothingness
And taught me e'en your cruelty to bless,
That cruelty which banished me the place

Where I, at least, had gazed upon your face.
And when no more I saw your beauty beam
The harsher yet your cruelty did seem;
Yet in obedience failed I not, and this
Hath been the means of compassing my bliss.
For Time, love's parent, pitiful at last,
Upon my woe commiserate eyes hath cast,
And done to me so excellent a turn,
That, if I now come back, think not I yearn
To sigh and dally, and renew the spell—
I only come to bid a last farewell.

Time, the revealer, hath not failed to prove
How base and sorry is all human love,
So that through Time, I now that time regret
When all my fancy upon love was set,
For then Time wasted was, lost in love's chains,
Sorrow whereof is all that now remains.
And Time in teaching me that love's deceit
Hath brought another, far more pure and sweet,
To dwell within me, in the lonely spot
Where tears and silence long have been my lot.
Time, to my heart, that higher love hath brought
With which the lower can no more be sought;
Time hath the latter into exile driven,
And, to the first, myself hath wholly given,
And consecrated to its service true
The heart and hand I erst had given to you.

When I was yours you nothing showed of grace,
And I that nothing loved, for your fair face;
Then, death for loyalty, you sought to give,
And I, in fleeing it, have learnt to live.
For, by the tender love that Time hath brought
The other vanquished is, and turned to nought;
Once did it lure and lull me, but I swear
It now hath wholly vanished in thin air.
And so your love and you I gladly leave,

And, needing neither, will forbear to grieve;
The other perfect, lasting love is mine,
To it I turn, nor for the lost one pine.

My leave I take of cruelty and pain,
Of hatred, bitter torment, cold disdain,
And those hot flames which fill you, and which fire
Him, that beholds your beauty, with desire.
Nor can I better part from ev'ry throe,
From ev'ry evil hap, and stress of woe,
And the fierce passion of love's awful hell,
Than by this single utterance: Farewell.
Learn therefore, that whate'er may be in store,
Each other's faces we shall see no more."

This letter was not read without many tears and much astonishment on the Queen's part, together with regret surpassing belief; for the loss of a lover filled with so perfect a love must needs have been keenly felt; and not all her treasures, nor even her kingdom itself, could hinder the Queen from being the poorest and most wretched lady in the world, seeing that she had lost that which all the world's wealth could not replace. And having heard mass to the end and returned to her apartment, she there made such mourning as her cruelty had provoked. And there was not a mountain, a rock or a forest to which she did not send in quest of the hermit; but He who had withdrawn him out of her hands preserved him from falling into them again, and took him away to Paradise before she could gain tidings of him in this world.

"This instance shows that a lover should never acknowledge that which may do him harm and in no wise help him. And still less, ladies, should you in your incredulity demand so hard a test, lest in getting your proof you lose your lover."

"Truly, Dagoucin," said Geburon, "I had all my life long deemed the lady of your story to be the most virtuous in the world, but now I hold her for the most cruel woman that ever lived."

"Nevertheless," said Parlamente, "it seems to me that she did him no wrong in wishing to try him for seven years, in order to see whether he did love her as much as he said. Men are so wont to speak falsely in these matters that before trusting them, if indeed one trust them at all, one cannot put them to the proof too long."

"The ladies of our day," said Hircan, "are far wiser than those of past times, for they are as sure of a lover after a seven days' trial as the others were after seven years."

"Yet there are those in this company," said Longarine, "who have been loved with all earnestness for seven years and more, and albeit have not been won."

"'Fore God," said Simontault, "you speak the truth; but such as they ought to be ranked with the ladies of former times, for they cannot be recognised as belonging to the present."

"After all," said Oisille, "the gentleman was much beholden to the lady, for it was owing to her that he devoted his heart wholly to God."

"It was very fortunate for him," said Saffredent, "that he found God upon the way, for, considering the grief he was in, I am surprised that he did not give himself to the devil."

"And did you give yourself to such a master," asked Ennasuite, "when your lady ill used you?"

"Yes, thousands of times," said Saffredent, "but the devil, seeing that all the torments of hell could bring me no more suffering than those which she caused me to endure, never condescended to take me. He knew full well that no devil is so bad as a lady who is deeply loved and will make no return."

"If I were you," said Parlamente to Saffredent, "and held such an opinion as that, I would never make love to woman."

"My affection," said Saffredent, "and my folly are always so great, that where I cannot command I am well content to serve. All the ill-will of the ladies cannot subdue the love that I bear them. But, I pray you, tell me on your conscience, do you praise this lady for such great harshness?"

"Ay," said Oisille, "I do, for I think that she wished neither to receive love nor to bestow it."

"If such was her mind," said Simontault, "why did she hold out to him the hope of being loved after the seven years were past?"

"I am of your opinion," said Longarine, "for ladies who are unwilling to love give no occasion for the continuance of the love that is offered them."

"Perhaps," said Nomerfide, "she loved some one else less worthy than that honourable gentleman, and so forsook the better for the worse."

"'T faith," said Saffredent, "I think that she meant to keep him in readiness and take him whenever she might leave the other whom for the time she loved the best."

"I can see," said Oisille, (4) "that the more we talk in this way, the more those who would not be harshly treated will do their utmost to speak ill of us. Wherefore, Dagoucin, I pray you give some lady your vote."

4 Prior to this sentence the following passage occurs in the De Thou MS.: "When Madame Oysille saw that the men, under pretence of censuring the Queen of Castille for conduct which certainly cannot be praised either in her or in any other, continued saying so much evil of women, that the most discreet and virtuous were spared no more than the most foolish and wanton, she could endure it no longer, but spoke and said," &c.—L.

"I give it," he said, "to Longarine, for I feel sure that she will tell us no melancholy story, and that she will speak the truth without sparing man or woman."

"Since you deem me so truthful," said Longarine, "I will be so bold as to relate an adventure that befel a very great Prince, who surpasses in worth all others of his time. Lying and dissimulation are, indeed, things not to be employed save in cases of extreme necessity; they are foul and infamous vices, more especially in Princes and great lords, on whose lips and features truth sits more becomingly than on those of other men. But no Prince in the world however great he be, even though he have all the honours and wealth he may desire, can escape being subject to the empire and tyranny of Love; indeed it would seem that the nobler and more high-minded the Prince, the more does Love strive to bring him under his mighty hand. For this glorious God sets no store by common things; his majesty rejoices solely in the daily working of miracles, such as weakening the strong, strengthening the weak, giving knowledge to the simple, taking intelligence from the most learned, favouring the passions, and overthrowing the reason. In such transformations as these does the Deity of Love delight. Now since Princes are not exempt from love's thraldom, so also are they not free from its necessities, and must therefore perforce be permitted to employ falsehood, hypocrisy and deceit, which, according to the teaching of Master Jehan de Mehun, (5) are the means to be employed for vanquishing our enemies. And, since such conduct is praiseworthy on the part of a Prince in such a case as this (though in any other it were deserving of blame), I will relate to you the devices to which a young Prince resorted, and by which he contrived to deceive those who are wont to deceive the whole world."

5 John dc Melun, who continued the Roman de la Rose begun by Lorris.—D.

[The Advocate's Wife attending on the Prince]

TALE XXV

A young Prince, whilst pretending to visit his lawyer and talk with him of his affairs, conversed so freely with the lawyer's wife, that he obtained from her what he desired.

In the city of Paris there dwelt an advocate who was more highly thought of than any other of his condition, (1) and who, being sought after by every one on account of his excellent parts, had become the richest of all those who wore the gown.

1 In five of the oldest MSS. of the Heptameron, and in the original editions of 1558, 1559, and 1560, the words are "than nine others of his condition." The explanation of this is, that the advocate's name, as ascertained by Baron Jerome Pichon, was Disome, which, written Dix-hommes, would literally mean "ten men." Baron Pichon has largely elucidated this story, and the essential points of his notice, contributed to the Mélanges de la Société des Bibliophiles Français, will be found summarized in the Appendix to this volume, B.—Ed.

Now, although he had had no children by his first wife, he was in hopes of having some by a second; for, although his body was no longer hearty, his heart and hopes were as much alive as ever. Accordingly, he made choice of one of the fairest maidens in the city; she was between eighteen and nineteen years of age, very handsome both in features and complexion, and still more handsome in figure. He loved her and treated her as well as could be; but he had no children by her any more than by his first wife, and this at last made her unhappy. And as youth cannot endure grief, she sought diversion away from home, and betook herself to dances and feasts; yet she did this in so seemly a fashion that her husband could not take it ill, for she was always in the company of women in whom he had trust.

One day, when she was at a wedding, there was also present a Prince of very high degree, who, when telling me the story, forbade me to discover his name. I may, however, tell you that he was the handsomest and most graceful Prince that has ever been or, in my opinion, ever will be in this realm. (2)

2 Francis L, prior to his accession.—Ed.

The Prince, seeing this fair and youthful lady whose eyes and countenance invited him to love her, came and spoke to her with such eloquence and grace that she was well pleased with his discourse.

Nor did she seek to hide from him that she had long had in her heart the love for which he prayed, but entreated that he would spare all pains to persuade her to a thing to which love, at first sight, had brought her to consent. Having, by the artlessness of love, so promptly gained what was well worth the pains of being won by time, the young Prince thanked God for His favour, and forthwith contrived matters so well that they agreed together in devising a means for seeing each other in private.

The young Prince failed not to appear at the time and place that had been agreed upon, and, that he might not injure his lady's honour, he went in disguise. On account, however, of the evil fellows (3) who were wont to prowl at night through the city, and to whom he cared not to make himself known, he took with him certain gentlemen in whom he trusted.

3 The French expression here is mauvais garsons, a name generally given to foot-pads at that time, but applied more particularly to a large band of brigands who, in the confusion prevailing during Francis I.'s captivity in Spain, began to infest the woods and forests around Paris, whence at night-time they descended upon the city. Several engagements were fought between them and the troops of the Queen-Regent, and although their leader, called King Guillot, was captured and hanged, the remnants of the band continued their depredations for several years.—B. J.

And on entering the street in which the lady lived, he parted from them, saying—

"If you hear no noise within a quarter of an hour, go home again, and come back here for me at about three or four o'clock."

They did as they were commanded, and, hearing no noise, withdrew.

The young Prince went straight to his advocate's house, where he found the door open as had been promised him. But as he was ascending the staircase he met the husband, carrying a candle in his hand, and was perceived by him before he was aware. However Love, who provides wit and boldness to contend with the difficulties that he creates, prompted the young Prince to go straight up to him and say—

"Master advocate, you know the trust which I and all belonging to my house have ever put in you, and how I reckon you among my best and truest servants. I have now thought it well to visit you here in private, both to commend my affairs to you, and also to beg you to give me something to drink, for I am in great thirst. And, I pray you, tell none that I have come here, for from this place I must go to another where I would not be known."

The worthy advocate was well pleased at the honour which the Prince paid him in coming thus privately to his house, and, leading him to his own room, he bade his wife prepare a collation of the best fruits and confections that she had.

Although the garments she wore, a kerchief and mantle, made her appear more beautiful than ever, the young Prince affected not to look at her or notice her, but spoke unceasingly to her husband about his affairs, as to one who had long had them in his hands. And, whilst the lady was kneeling with the confections before the Prince, and her husband was gone to the sideboard in order to serve him with drink, she told him that on leaving the room he must not fail to enter a closet which he would find on the right hand, and whither she would very soon come to see him.

As soon as he had drunk, he thanked the advocate, who was all eagerness to attend him; but the Prince assured him that in the place whither he was going he had no need of attendance, and thereupon turning to the wife, he said—

"Moreover, I will not do so ill as to deprive you of your excellent husband, who is also an old servant of mine. Well may you render thanks to God since you are so fortunate as to have such a husband, well may you render him service and obedience. If you did otherwise, you would be blameworthy indeed."

With these virtuous words the young Prince went away, and, closing the door behind him so that he might not be followed to the staircase, he entered the closet, whither also came the fair lady as soon as her husband had fallen asleep.

Thence she led the Prince into a cabinet as choicely furnished as might be, though in truth there were no fairer figures in it than he and she, no matter what garments they may have been pleased to wear. And here, I doubt not, she kept word with him as to all that she had promised.

He departed thence at the hour which he had appointed with his gentlemen, and found them at the spot where he had aforetime bidden them wait.

As this intercourse lasted a fairly long time, the young Prince chose a shorter way to the advocate's house, and this led him through a monastery of monks. (4) And so well did he contrive matters with the Prior, that the porter used always to open the gate for him about midnight, and do the like also when he returned. And, as the house which he visited was hard by, he used to take nobody with him.

4 If at this period Jane Disome, the heroine of the story, lived in the Rue de la Pauheminerie, where she is known to have died some years afterwards, this monastery, in Baron Jerome Pichon's opinion, would be the Blancs-Manteaux, in the Marais district of Paris. We may further point out that in the Rue Barbette, near by, there was till modern times a house traditionally known as the "hôtel de la belle Féronnière." That many writers have confused the heroine of this tale with La Belle Féronnière (so called because her husband was a certain Le Féron, an advocate) seems manifest; the intrigue in which the former took part was doubtless ascribed in error to the latter, and the proximity of their abodes may have led to the mistake. It should be pointed out, however, that the amour here recorded by Queen Margaret took place in or about the year 1515, before Francis I. ascended the throne, whereas La Féronnière was in all her beauty between 1530 and 1540. The tradition that the King had an intrigue with La Féronnière reposes on the flimsiest evidence (see Appendix B), and the supposition, re-echoed by the Bibliophile Jacob, that it was carried on in the Rue de l'Hirondelle, is entirely erroneous. The house, adorned with the salamander device and corneted initials of Francis I., which formerly extended from that street to the Rue Git-le-Coeur, never had any connection with La Féronnière. It was the famous so-called Palace of Love which the King built for his acknowledged mistress, Anne de Pisseleu, Duchess of Étampes.—Ed.

Although he led the life that I have described, he was nevertheless a Prince that feared and loved God, and although he made no pause when going, he never failed on his return to continue for a long time praying in the church. And the monks, who when going to and fro at the hour of matins used to see him there on his knees, were thereby led to consider him the holiest man alive.

This Prince had a sister (5) who often visited this monastery, and as she loved her brother more than any other living being, she used to commend him to the prayers of all whom she knew to be good.

5 This of course is Queen Margaret, then Duchess of Alençon. On account of her apparent intimacy with the prior, M. de Montaiglon conjectures that the monastery may have been that of St. Martin-in-the-Fields.—See ante, Tale XXII.—Ed.

One day, when she was in this manner commending him lovingly to the Prior of the monastery, the Prior said to her—

"Ah, madam, whom are you thus commending to me? You are speaking to me of a man in whose prayers, above those of all others, I would myself fain be remembered. For if he be not a holy man and a just"—here he quoted the passage which says, "Blessed is he that can do evil and doeth it not"—"*I* cannot hope to be held for such."

The sister, wishing to learn what knowledge this worthy father could have of her brother's goodness, questioned him so pressingly that he at last told her the secret under the seal of the confessional, saying—

"Is it not an admirable thing to see a young and handsome Prince forsake pleasure and repose in order to come so often to hear our matins? Nor comes he like a Prince seeking honour of men, but quite alone, like a simple monk, and hides himself in one of our chapels. Truly such piety so shames both the monks and me, that we do not deem ourselves worthy of being called men of religion in comparison with him."

When the sister heard these words she was at a loss what to think. She knew that, although her brother was worldly enough, he had a tender conscience, as well as great faith and love towards God; but she had never suspected him of a leaning towards any superstitions or rites save such as a good Christian should observe. (6) She therefore went to him and told him the good opinion that the monks had of him, whereat he could not hold from laughing, and in such a manner that she, knowing him as she did her own heart, perceived that there was something hidden beneath his devotion; whereupon she rested not until she had made him tell her the truth.

6 In Boaistuau's edition this sentence ends, "But she had never suspected him of going to church at such an hour as this."—L.

And she has made me here set it down in writing, for the purpose, ladies, of showing you that there is no lawyer so crafty and no monk so shrewd, but love, in case of need, gives the power of tricking them both, to those whose sole experience is in truly loving. And since love can thus deceive the deceivers, well may we, who are simple and ignorant folk, stand in awe of him.

"Although," said Geburon, "I can pretty well guess who the young Prince is, I must say that in this matter he was worthy of praise. We meet with few great lords who reck aught of a woman's honour or a public scandal, if only they have their pleasure; nay, they are often well pleased to have men believe something that is even worse than the truth."

"Truly," said Oisille, "I could wish that all young lords would follow his example, for the scandal is often worse than the sin."

"Of course," said Nomerfide, "the prayers he offered up at the monastery through which he passed were sincere."

"That is not a matter for you to judge," said Parlamente, "for perhaps his repentance on his return was great enough to procure him the pardon of his sin."

"'Tis a hard matter," said Hircan, "to repent of an offence so pleasing. For my own part I have many a time confessed such a one, but seldom have I repented of it."

"It would be better," said Oisille, "not to confess at all, if one do not sincerely repent."

"Well, madam," said Hircan, "sin sorely displeases me, and I am grieved to offend God, but, for all that, such sin is ever a pleasure to me."

"You and those like you," said Parlamente, "would fain have neither God nor law other than your own desires might set up."

"I will own to you," said Hircan, "that I would gladly have God take as deep a pleasure in my pleasures as I do myself, for I should then often give Him occasion to rejoice."

"However, you cannot set up a new God," said Geburon, "and so we must e'en obey the one we have. Let us therefore leave such disputes to theologians, and allow Longarine to give some one her vote."

"I give it," she said, "to Saffredent, but I will beg him to tell us the finest tale he can think of, and not to be so intent on speaking evil of women as to hide the truth when there is something good of them to relate."

"In sooth," said Saffredent, "I consent, for I have here in hand the story of a wanton woman and a discreet one, and you shall take example by her who pleases you best. You will see that just as love leads wicked people to do wicked things, so does it lead a virtuous heart to do things that are worthy of praise; for love in itself is good, although the evil that is in those that are subject to it often makes it take a new title, such as wanton, light, cruel or vile. However, you will see from the tale that I am now about to relate that love does not change the heart, but discovers it to be what it really is, wanton in the wanton and discreet in the discreet."

[The Lord of Avannes paying His Court in Disguise]

TALE XXVI

By the counsel and sisterly affection of a virtuous lady, the Lord of Avannes was drawn from the wanton love that he entertained for a gentlewoman dwelling at Pampeluna.

In the days of King Louis the Twelfth there lived a young lord called Monsieur d'Avannes, (1) son of the Lord of Albret [and] brother to King John of Navarre, with whom this aforesaid Lord of Avannes commonly abode.

1 This is Gabriel d'Albret, Lord of Avesnes and Lesparre, fourth son of Alan the Great, Sire d'Albret, and brother of John d'Albret, King of Navarre, respecting whom see post, note 4 to Tale XXX. Queen Margaret is in error in dating this story from the reign of Louis XII. The incidents she relates must have occurred between 1485 and 1490, under the reign of Charles VIII., by whom Gabriel d'Albret, on reaching manhood, was successively appointed counsellor and chamberlain, Seneschal of Guyenne and Viceroy of Naples. Under Louis XII. he took a prominent part in the Italian campaigns of 1500-1503, in which latter year he is known to have made his will, bequeathing all he possessed to his brother, Cardinal d'Albret. He died a bachelor in 1504.—See Anselme's Histoire Généalogique, vol. vi. p. 214.—L. and Ed.

Now this young lord, who was fifteen years of age, was so handsome and so fully endowed with every excellent grace that he seemed to have been made solely to be loved and admired, as he was indeed by all who saw him, and above all by a lady who dwelt in the town of Pampeluna (2) in Navarre. She was married to a very rich man, with whom she lived in all virtue, inasmuch that, although her husband was nearly fifty years old and she was only three and twenty, she dressed so plainly that she had more the appearance of a widow than of a married woman. Moreover, she was never known to go to weddings or feasts unless accompanied by her husband, whose worth and virtue she prized so highly that she set them before all the comeliness of other men. And her husband, finding her so discreet, trusted her and gave all the affairs of his household into her hands.

2 Pampeluna or Pamplona, the capital of Navarre, wrested from King John in 1512 by the troops of Ferdinand the Catholic.—Ed.

One day this rich man was invited with his wife to a wedding among their kinsfolk; and among those who were present to do honour to the bridal was the young Lord of Avannes, who was exceedingly fond of dancing, as was natural in one who surpassed therein all others of his time. When dinner was over and the dances were begun, the rich man begged the Lord of Avannes to do his part, whereupon the said lord asked him with whom he would have him dance.

"My lord," replied the gentleman, "I can present to you no lady fairer and more completely at my disposal than my wife, and I therefore beg you to honour me so far as to lead her out."

This the young Prince did; and he was still so young that he took far greater pleasure in frisking and dancing than in observing the beauty of the ladies. But his partner, on the contrary, gave more heed to his grace and beauty than to the dance, though in her prudence she took good care not to let this appear.

The supper hour being come, the Lord of Avannes bade the company farewell, and departed to the castle, (3) whither the rich man accompanied him on his mule. And as they were going, the rich man said to him—

"My lord, you have this day done so much honour to my kinsfolk and to me, that I should indeed be ungrateful if I did not place myself with all that belongs to me at your service. I know, sir, that lords like yourself, who have stern and miserly fathers, are often in greater need of money than we, who, with small establishments and careful husbandry, seek only to save up wealth. Now, albeit God has given me a wife after my own heart, it has not pleased Him to give me all my Paradise in this world, for He has withheld from me the joy that fathers derive from having children. I know, my lord, that it is not for me to adopt you as a son, but if you will accept me for your servant and make known to me your little affairs, I will not fail to assist you in your need so far as a hundred thousand crowns may go."

3 Evidently the castle of Pampeluna, where Gabriel d'Albret resided with his brother the King.—Ed.

The Lord of Avannes was in great joy at this offer, for he had just such a father as the other had described; accordingly he thanked him, and called him his adopted father.

From that hour the rich man evinced so much love towards the Lord of Avannes, that morning and evening he failed not to inquire whether he had need of anything, nor did he conceal this devotion from his wife, who loved him for it twice as much as before. Thenceforward the Lord of Avannes had no lack of anything that he desired. He often visited the rich man, and ate and drank with him; and when he found the husband abroad, the wife gave him all that he required, and further spoke to him so sagely, exhorting him to live discreetly and virtuously, that he reverenced and loved her above all other women.

Having God and honour before her eyes, she remained content with thus seeing him and speaking to him, for these are sufficient for virtuous and honourable love; and she never gave any token whereby he might have imagined that she felt aught but a sisterly and Christian affection towards him.

While this secret love continued, the Lord of Avannes, who, by the assistance that I have spoken of, was always well and splendidly apparelled, came to the age of seventeen years, and began to frequent the company of ladies more than had been his wont. And although he would fain have loved this virtuous lady rather than any other, yet his fear of losing her friendship should she hear any such discourse from him, led him to remain silent and to divert himself elsewhere.

He therefore addressed himself to a gentlewoman of the neighbourhood of Pampeluna, who had a house in the town, and was married to a young man whose chief delight was in horses, hawks and hounds. For her sake, he began to set on foot a thousand diversions, such as tourneys, races, wrestlings, masquerades, banquets, and other pastimes, at all of which this young lady was present. But as her husband was very humorsome, and her parents, knowing her to be both fair and frolicsome, were jealous of her honour, they kept such strict watch over her that my Lord of Avannes could obtain nothing from her save a word or two at the dance, although, from the little that had passed between them, he well knew that time and place alone were wanting to crown their loves.

He therefore went to his good father, the rich man, and told him that he deeply desired to make a pilgrimage to our Lady of Montferrat, (4) for which reason he begged him to house his followers, seeing that he wished to go alone.

4 The famous monastery of Montserrate, at eight leagues from Barcelona, where is preserved the ebony statue of the Virgin carrying the Infant Jesus, which is traditionally said to have been carved by St. Luke, and to have been brought to Spain by St. Peter.—See Libro de la historia y milagros hechos à invocation de Nuestra Seilora de Montserrate, Barcelona, 1556, 8vo.—Ed.

To this the rich man agreed; but his wife, in whose heart was that great soothsayer, Love, forthwith suspected the true nature of the journey, and could not refrain from saying—

"My lord, my lord, the Lady you adore is not without the walls of this town, so I pray that you will have in all matters a care for your health."

At this he, who both feared and loved her, blushed so deeply that, without speaking a word, he confessed the truth; and so he went away.

Having bought a couple of handsome Spanish horses, he dressed himself as a groom, and disguised his face in such a manner that none could know him. The gentleman who was husband to the wanton lady, and who loved horses more than aught beside, saw the two that the Lord of Avannes was leading, and forthwith offered to buy them. When he had done so, he looked at the groom, who was managing the horses excellently well, and asked whether he would enter his service. The Lord of Avannes replied that he would; saying that he was but a poor groom, who knew no trade except the caring of horses, but in this he could do so well that he would assuredly give satisfaction. At this the gentleman was pleased, and having given him the charge of all his horses, entered his house, and told his wife that he was leaving for the castle, and confided his horses and groom to her keeping.

The lady, as much to please her husband as for her own diversion, went to see the horses, and looked at the new groom, who seemed to her to be well favoured, though she did not at all recognise him. Seeing that he was not recognised, he came up to do her reverence in the Spanish fashion and kissed her hand, and, in doing so, pressed it so closely that she at once knew him, for he had often done the same at the dance. From that moment, the lady thought of nothing but how she might speak to him in private; and contrived to do so that very evening, for, being invited to a banquet, to which her husband wished to take her, she pretended that she was ill and unable to go.

The husband, being unwilling to disappoint his friends, thereupon said to her—

"Since you will not come, my love, I pray you take good care of my horses and hounds, so that they may want for nothing."

The lady deemed this charge a very agreeable one, but, without showing it, she replied that since he had nothing better for her to do, she would show him even in these trifling matters how much she desired to please him.

And scarcely was her husband outside the door than she went down to the stable, where she found that something was amiss, and to set it right gave so many orders to the serving-men on this side and the other, that at last she was left alone with the chief groom, when, fearing that some one might come upon them, she said to him—

"Go into the garden, and wait for me in a summer house that stands at the end of the alley."

This he did, and with such speed that he stayed not even to thank her.

When she had set the whole stable in order, she went to see the dogs, and was so careful to have them properly treated, that from mistress she seemed to have become a serving-woman. Afterwards she withdrew to her own apartment, where she lay down weariedly upon the bed, saying that she wished to rest. All her women left her excepting one whom she trusted, and to whom she said—

"Go into the garden, and bring here the man whom you will find at the end of the alley."

The maid went and found the groom, whom she forthwith brought to the lady, and the latter then sent her outside to watch for her husband's return. When the Lord of Avannes found himself alone with the lady, he doffed his groom's dress, took off his false nose and beard, and, not like a timorous groom, but like the handsome lord he was, boldly got into bed with her without so much as asking her leave; and he was received as the handsomest youth of his time deserved to be by the handsomest and gayest lady in the land, and remained with her until her husband returned. Then he again took his mask and left the place which his craft and artifice had usurped.

On entering the courtyard the gentleman heard of the diligence that his wife had shown in obeying him, and he thanked her heartily for it.

"Sweetheart," said the lady, "I did but my duty. Tis true that if we did not keep watch upon these rogues of servants you would not have a dog without the mange or a horse in good condition; but, now that I know their slothfulness and your wishes, you shall be better served than ever you were before."

The gentleman, who thought that he had chosen the best groom in the world, asked her what she thought of him.

"I will own, sir," she replied, "that he does his work as well as any you could have chosen, but he needs to be urged on, for he is the sleepiest knave I ever saw."

So the lord and his lady lived together more lovingly than before, and he lost all the suspicion and jealousy with which he had regarded her, seeing that she was now as careful of her house hold as she had formerly been devoted to banquets, dances and assemblies. Whereas, also, she had formerly been wont to spend four hours in attiring herself, she was now often content to wear nothing but a dressing-gown over her chemise; and for this she was praised by her husband and by every one else, for they did not understand that a stronger devil had entered her and thrust out a weaker one.

Thus did this young lady, under the guise of a virtuous woman, like the hypocrite she was, live in such wantonness that reason, conscience, order and moderation found no place within her. The youth and tender constitution of the Lord of Avannes could not long endure this, and he began to grow so pale and lean that even without his mask he might well have passed unrecognised; yet the mad love that he had for this woman so blunted his understanding that he imagined he had strength to accomplish feats that even Hercules had tried in vain. However, being at last constrained by sickness and advised thereto by his lady, who was not so fond of him sick as sound, he asked his master's leave to return home, and this his master gave him with much regret, making him promise to come back to service when he was well again.

In this wise did the Lord of Avannes go away, and all on foot, for he had only the length of a street to travel. On arriving at the house of his good father, the rich man, he there found only his wife, whose honourable love for him had been in no whit lessened by his journey. But when she saw him so colourless and thin, she could not refrain from saying to him—

"I do not know, my lord, how your conscience may be, but your body has certainly not been bettered by your pilgrimage. I fear me that your journeyings by night have done you more harm than your journeyings by day, for had you gone to Jerusalem on foot you would have come back more sunburnt, indeed, but not so thin and weak. Pay good heed to this one, and worship no longer such images as those, which, instead of reviving the dead, cause the living to die. I would say more, but if your body has sinned it has been well punished, and I feel too much pity for you to add any further distress."

When my Lord of Avannes heard these words, he was as sorry as he was ashamed.

"Madam," he replied, "I have heard that repentance follows upon sin, and now I have proved it to my cost. But I pray you pardon my youth, which could not have been punished save by the evil in which it would not believe."

Thereupon changing her discourse, the lady made him lie down in a handsome bed, where he remained for a fortnight, taking nothing but restoratives; and the lady and her husband constantly kept him company, so that he always had one or the other beside him. And although he had acted foolishly, as you have heard, contrary to the desire and counsel of the virtuous lady, she, nevertheless, lost nought of the virtuous love that she felt towards him, for she still hoped that, after spending his early youth in follies, he would throw them off and bring himself to love virtuously, and so be all her own.

During the fortnight that he was in her house, she held to him such excellent discourse, all tending to the love of virtue, that he began to loathe the folly that he had committed. Observing, moreover, the lady's beauty, which surpassed that of the wanton one, and becoming more and more aware of the graces and virtues that were in her, he one day, when it was rather dark, could not longer hold from speaking, but, putting away all fear, said to her—

"I see no better means, madam, for becoming a virtuous man such as you urge me and desire me to be, than by being heart and soul in love with virtue. I therefore pray you, madam, to tell me whether you will give me in this matter all the assistance and favour that you can."

The lady rejoiced to find him speaking in this way, and replied—

"I promise you, my lord, that if you are in love with virtue as it beseems a lord like yourself to be, I will assist your efforts with all the strength that God has given me."

"Now, madam," said my Lord of Avannes, "remember your promise, and consider also that God, whom man knows by faith alone, deigned to take a fleshly nature like that of the sinner upon Himself, in order that, by drawing our flesh to the love of His humanity, He might at the same time draw our spirits to the love of His divinity, thus making use of visible means to make us in all faith love the things which are invisible. In like manner this virtue, which I would fain love all my life long, is a thing invisible except in so far as it produces outward effects, for which reason it must take some bodily shape in order to become known among men. And this it has done by clothing itself in your form, the most perfect it could find. I therefore recognise and own that you are not only virtuous but virtue itself; and now, finding it shine beneath the veil of the most perfect person that was ever known, I would fain serve it and honour it all my life, renouncing for its sake every other vain and vicious love."

The lady, who was no less pleased than surprised to hear these words, concealed her happiness and said—

"My lord, I will not undertake to answer your theology, but since I am more ready to apprehend evil than to believe in good, I will entreat you to address to me no more such words as lead you to esteem but lightly those who are wont to believe them. I very well know that I am a woman like any other and imperfect, and that virtue would do a greater thing by transforming me into itself than by assuming my form—unless, indeed, it would fain pass unrecognised through the world, for in such a garb as mine its real nature could never be known. Nevertheless, my lord, with all my imperfections, I have ever borne to you all such affection as is right and possible in a woman who reverences God and her honour. But this affection shall not be declared until your heart is capable of that patience which a virtuous love enjoins. At that time, my lord, I shall know what to say, but meanwhile be assured that you do not love your own welfare, person and honour as I myself love them."

The Lord of Avannes timorously and with tears in his eyes entreated her earnestly to seal her words with a kiss, but she refused, saying that she would not break for him the custom of her country.

While this discussion was going on the husband came in, and my Lord of Avannes said to him—

"I am greatly indebted, father, both to you and to your wife, and I pray you ever to look upon me as your son."

This the worthy man readily promised.

"And to seal your love," said the Lord of Avannes, "I pray you let me kiss you." This he did, after which the Lord of Avannes said—:

"If I were not afraid of offending against the law, I would do the same to your wife and my mother."

Upon this, the husband commanded his wife to kiss him, which she did without appearing either to like or to dislike what her husband commanded her. But the fire that words had already kindled in the poor lord's heart, grew fiercer at this kiss which had been so earnestly sought for and so cruelly denied.

After this the Lord of Avannes betook himself to the castle to see his brother, the King, to whom he told fine stories about his journey to Montferrat. He found that the King was going to Oly and Taffares, (5) and, reflecting that the journey would be a long one, he fell into deep sadness, and resolved before going away to try whether the virtuous lady were not better disposed towards him than she appeared to be.

5 Evidently Olite and Tafalla, the former at thirty and the latter at twenty-seven miles from Pamplona. The two towns were commonly called la flor de Navarra. King John doubtless intended sojourning at the summer palaces which his predecessor Carlos the Noble had built at either locality, and which were connected, it is said, by a gallery a league in length. Some ruins of these palaces still exist. —Ed.

He therefore went to lodge in the street in which she lived, where he hired an old house, badly built of timber. About midnight he set fire to it, and the alarm, which spread through the whole town, reached the rich man's house. He asked from the window where the fire was, and hearing that it was in the house of the Lord of Avannes, immediately hastened thither with all his servants. He found the young lord in the street, clad in nothing but his shirt, whereat in his deep compassion he took him in his arms, and, covering him with his own robe, brought him home as quickly as possible, where he said to his wife, who was in bed—

"Here, sweetheart, I give this prisoner into your charge. Treat him as you would treat myself."

As soon as he was gone, the Lord of Avannes, who would gladly have been treated like a husband, sprang lightly into the bed, hoping that place and opportunity would bring this discreet lady to a different mind; but he found the contrary to be the case, for as he leaped into the bed on one side, she got out at the other. Then, putting on her dressing-gown, she came up to the head of the bed and spoke as follows—

"Did you think, my lord, that opportunity could influence a chaste heart? Nay, just as gold is tried in the furnace, so a chaste heart becomes stronger and more virtuous in the midst of temptation, and grows colder the more it is assailed by its opposite. You may be sure, therefore, that had I been otherwise minded than I professed myself to be, I should not have wanted means, to which I have paid no heed solely because I desire not to use them. So I beg of you, if you would have me preserve my affection for you, put away not merely the desire but even the thought that you can by any means whatever make me other than I am."

While she was speaking, her women came in, and she commanded a collation of all kinds of sweetmeats to be brought; but the young lord could neither eat nor drink, in such despair was he at having failed in his enterprise, and in such fear lest this manifestation of his passion should cost him the familiar intercourse that he had been wont to have with her.

Having dealt with the fire, the husband came back again, and begged the Lord of Avannes to remain at his house for the night. This he did, but in such wise that his eyes were more exercised in weeping than in sleeping. Early in the morning he went to bid them farewell, while they were still in bed; and in kissing the lady he perceived that she felt more pity for the offence than anger against the offender, and thus was another brand added to the fire of his love. After dinner, he set out for Taffares with the King; but before leaving he went again to take yet another farewell of his good father and the lady who, after her husband's first command, made no difficulty in kissing him as her son.

But you may be sure that the more virtue prevented her eyes and features from testifying to the hidden flame, the fiercer and more intolerable did that flame become. And so, being unable to endure the war between love and honour, which was waging in her heart, but which she had nevertheless resolved should never be made apparent, and no longer having the comfort of seeing and speaking to him for whose sake alone she cared to live, she fell at last into a continuous fever, caused by a melancholic humour which so wrought upon her that the extremities of her body became quite cold, while her inward parts burned without ceasing. The doctors, who have not the health of men in their power, began to grow very doubtful concerning her recovery, by reason of an obstruction that affected the extremities, and advised her husband to admonish her to think of her conscience and remember that she was in God's hands—as though indeed the healthy were not in them also.

The husband, who loved his wife devotedly, was so saddened by their words that for his comfort he wrote to the Lord of Avannes entreating him to take the trouble to come and see them, in the hope that the sight of him might be of advantage to the patient. On receiving the letter, the Lord of Avannes did not tarry, but started off post-haste to the house of his worthy father, where he found the servants, both men and women, assembled at the door, making such lament for their mistress as she deserved.

So greatly amazed was he at the sight, that he remained on the threshold like one paralysed, until he beheld his good father, who embraced him, weeping the while so bitterly that he could not utter a word. Then he led the Lord of Avannes to the chamber of the sick lady, who, turning her languid eyes upon him, put out her hand and drew him to her with all the strength she had. She kissed and embraced him, and made wondrous lamentation, saying—

"O my lord, the hour has come when all dissimulation must cease, and I must confess the truth which I have been at such pains to hide from you. If your affection for me was great, know that mine for you has been no less; but my grief has been greater than yours, because I have had the anguish of concealing it contrary to the wish of my heart. God and my honour have never, my lord, suffered me to make it known to you, lest I should increase in you that which I sought to diminish; but you must learn that the 'no' I so often said to you pained me so greatly in the utterance that it has indeed proved the cause of my death.

"Nevertheless, I am glad it should be so, and that God in His grace should have caused me to die before the vehemence of my love has stained my conscience and my fair fame; for smaller fires have ere now destroyed greater and stronger structures. And I am glad that before dying I have been able to make known to you that my affection is equal to your own, save only that men's honour and women's are not the same thing. And I pray you, my lord, fear not henceforward to address yourself to the greatest and most virtuous of ladies; for in such hearts do the deepest and discreetest passions dwell, and moreover, your own grace and beauty and worth will not suffer your love to toil without reward.

"I will not beg you, my lord, to pray God for me, because I know full well that the gate of Paradise is never closed against true lovers, and that the fire of love punishes lovers so severely in this life here that they are forgiven the sharp torment of Purgatory. And now, my lord, farewell; I commend to you your good father, my husband. Tell him the truth as you have heard it from me, that he may know how I have loved God and him. And come no more before my eyes, for I now desire to think only of obtaining those promises made to me by God before the creation of the world."

With these words she kissed him and embraced him with all the strength of her feeble arms. The young lord, whose heart was as nearly dead through pity as hers was through pain, was unable to say a single word. He withdrew from her sight to a bed that was in the room, and there several times swooned away.

Then the lady called her husband, and, after giving him much virtuous counsel, commended the Lord of Avannes to him, declaring that next to himself she had loved him more than any one upon earth, and so, kissing her husband, she bade him farewell. Then, after the extreme unction, the Holy Sacrament was brought to her from the altar, and this she received with the joy of one who is assured of her salvation. And finding that her sight was growing dim and her strength failing her, she began to utter the "In manus" aloud.

Hearing this cry, the Lord of Avannes raised himself up on the bed where he was lying, and gazing piteously upon her, beheld her with a gentle sigh surrender her glorious soul to Him from whom it had come. When he perceived that she was dead, he ran to the body, which when alive he had ever approached with fear, and kissed and embraced it in such wise that he could hardly be separated from it, whereat the husband was greatly astonished, for he had never believed he bore her so much affection; and with the words, "Tis too much, my lord," he led him away.

After he had lamented for a great while, the Lord of Avannes related all the converse they had had together during their love, and how, until her death, she had never given him sign of aught save severity. This, while it gave the husband exceeding joy, also increased his grief and sorrow at the loss he had sustained, and for the remainder of his days he rendered service to the Lord of Avannes.

But from that time forward my Lord of Avannes, who was then only eighteen years old, went to reside at Court, where he lived for many years without wishing to see or to speak with any living woman by reason of his grief for the lady he had lost; and he wore mourning for her sake during more than ten years. (6)

6 Some extracts from Brantôme bearing on this story will be found in the Appendix, C.

"You here see, ladies, what a difference there is between a wanton lady and a discreet one. The effects of love are also different in each case; for the one came by a glorious and praiseworthy death, while the other lived only too long with the reputation of a vile and shameless woman. Just as the death of a saint is precious in the sight of God, so is the death of a sinner abhorrent."

"In truth, Saffredent," said Oisille, "you have told us the finest tale imaginable, and any one who knew the hero would deem it better still. I have never seen a handsomer or more graceful gentleman than was this Lord of Avannes."

"She was indeed a very virtuous woman," said Saffredent. "So as to appear outwardly more virtuous than she was in her heart, and to conceal her love for this worthy lord which reason and nature had inspired, she must needs die rather than take the pleasure which she secretly desired."

"If she had felt such a desire," said Parlamente, "she would have lacked neither place nor opportunity to make it known; but the greatness of her virtue prevented her desire from exceeding the bounds of reason."

"You may paint her as you will," said Hircan, "but I know very well that a stronger devil always thrusts out the weaker, and that the pride of ladies seeks pleasure rather than the fear and love of God. Their robes are long and well woven with dissimulation, so that we cannot tell what is beneath, for if their honour were not more easily stained than ours, (7) you would find that

Nature's work is as complete in them as in ourselves. But not daring to take the pleasure they desire, they have exchanged that vice for a greater, which they deem more honourable, I mean a self-sufficient cruelty, whereby they look to obtain everlasting renown.

7 This reading is borrowed from MS. No. 1520. In the MS. mainly followed for this translation, the passage runs as follows-"if their honour were not more easily stained than their hearts."—L.

By thus glorying in their resistance to the vice of Nature's law—if, indeed, anything natural be vicious—they become not only like inhuman and cruel beasts, but even like the devils whose pride and subtility they borrow." (8)

8 This reading is borrowed from MS. No. 1520. In our MS. the passage runs—"like the devils whose semblance and subtility they borrow."—L.

"Tis a pity," said Nomerfide, "that you should have an honourable wife, for you not only think lightly of virtue, but are even fain to prove that it is vice."

"I am very glad," said Hircan, "to have a wife of good repute, just as I, myself, would be of good repute. But as for chastity of heart, I believe that we are both children of Adam and Eve; wherefore, when we examine ourselves, we have no need to cover our nakedness with leaves, but should rather confess our frailty."

"I know," said Parlamente, "that we all have need of God's grace, being all steeped in sin; but, for all that, our temptations are not similar to yours, and if we sin through pride, no one is injured by it, nor do our bodies and hands receive a stain. But your pleasure consists in dishonouring women, and your honour in slaying men in war—two things expressly contrary to the law of God." (9)

"I admit what you say," said Geburon, "but God has said, 'Whosoever looketh with lust, hath already committed adultery in his heart,' and further, 'Whosoever hateth his neighbour is a murderer.' (10) Do you think that women offend less against these texts than we?"

9 This sentence, defective in our MS., is taken from No. 1520.—L.

10 1 St. John iii. 15.—M.

"God, who judges the heart," said Longarine, "must decide that. But it is an important thing that men should not be able to accuse us, for the goodness of God is so great, that He will not judge us unless there be an accuser. And so well, moreover, does He know the frailty of our hearts, that He will even love us for not having put our thoughts into execution."

"I pray you," said Saffredent, "let us leave this dispute, for it savours more of a sermon than of a tale. I give my vote to Ennasuite, and beg that she will bear in mind to make us laugh."

"Indeed," said she, "I will not fail to do so; for I would have you know that whilst coming hither, resolved upon relating a fine story to you to-day, I was told so merry a tale about two servants of a Princess, that, in laughing at it, I quite forgot the melancholy story which I had prepared, and which I will put off until to-morrow; for, with the merry face I now have, you would scarce find it to your liking."

[The Secretary imploring the Lady not To Tell Of His Wickedness]

TALE XXVII

A secretary sought the wife of his host and comrade in dishonourable and unlawful love, and as she made show of willingly giving ear to him, he was persuaded that he had won her. But she was virtuous, and, while dissembling towards him, deceived his hopes and made known his viciousness to her husband. (1)

1 The incidents here related would have occurred at Amboise between 1540 and 1545. The hero of the story would probably be John Frotté, Queen Margaret's First Secretary, who also apparently figures in Tale XXVIII. The Sires de Frotté had been in the service of the Dukes of Alençon since the early part of the fifteenth century. Ste-Marthe says of John Frotté that he was a man of great experience and good wit, prudent, dutiful and diligent. He died secretary to Francis I.—L. and B. J.

In the town of Amboise there lived one of this Princess's servants, an honest man who served her in the quality of valet-de-chambre, and who used readily to entertain those that visited his house, more especially his own comrades; and not long since one of his mistress's servants came to lodge with him, and remained with him ten or twelve days.

This man was so ugly that he looked more like a King of the cannibals than a Christian, and although his host treated him as a friend and a brother, and with all the courtesy imaginable, he behaved in return not only like one who has forgotten all honour, but as one who has never had it in his heart. For he sought, in dishonourable and unlawful love, his comrade's wife, who was in no sort attractive to lust but rather the reverse, and was moreover as virtuous a woman as any in the town in which she lived. When she perceived the man's evil intent, she thought it better to employ dissimulation in order to bring his viciousness to light, rather than conceal it by a sudden refusal; and she therefore made a pretence of approving his discourse. He then believed he had won her, and, paying no heed to her age, which was that of fifty years, or to her lack of beauty, or her reputation as a virtuous woman attached to her husband, he urged his suit continually.

One day, the husband being in the house, the wife and her suitor were in a large room together, when she pretended that he had but to find some safe spot in order to have such private converse with her as he desired. He immediately replied that it was only necessary to go up to the garret. She instantly rose, and begged him to go first, saying that she would follow. Smiling with as sweet a countenance as that of a big baboon entertaining a friend, he went lightly up the stairway; and, on the tip-toe of expectation with regard to that which he so greatly desired, burning with a fire not clear, like that of juniper, but dense like that of coal in the furnace, he listened whether she was coming after him. But instead of hearing her footsteps, he heard her voice saying—

"Wait, master secretary, for a little; I am going to find out whether it be my husband's pleasure that I should go up to you."

His face when laughing was ugly indeed, and you may imagine, ladies, how it looked when he wept; but he came down instantly, with tears in his eyes, and besought her for the love of God not to say aught that would destroy the friendship between his comrade and himself.

"I am sure," she replied, "that you like him too well to say anything he may not hear. I shall therefore go and tell him of the matter."

And this, in spite of all his entreaties and threats, she did. And if his shame thereat was great as he fled the place, the husband's joy was no less on hearing of the honourable deception that his wife had practised; indeed, so pleased was he with his wife's virtue that he took no notice of his comrade's viciousness, deeming him sufficiently punished inasmuch as the shame he had thought to work in another's household had fallen upon his own head.

"I think that from this tale honest people should learn not to admit to their houses those whose conscience, heart and understanding know nought of God, honour and true love."

"Though your tale be short," said Oisille, "it is as pleasant as any I have heard, and it is to the honour of a virtuous woman."

"'Fore God," said Simontault, "it is no great honour for a virtuous woman to refuse a man so ugly as you represent this secretary to have been. Had he been handsome and polite, her virtue would then have been clear. I think I know who he is, and, if it were my turn, I could tell you another story about him that is no less droll."

"Let that be no hindrance," said Ennasuite, "for I give you my vote."

Thereupon Simontault began as follows:—

"Those who are accustomed to dwell at Court or in large towns value their own knowledge so highly that they think very little of all other men in comparison with themselves; but, for all that, there are subtle and crafty folk to be found in every condition of life. Still, when those who think themselves the cleverest are caught tripping, their pride makes the jest a particularly pleasant one, and this I will try to show by telling you of something that lately happened."

[The Secretary Opening the Pasty]

TALE XXVIII

A secretary, thinking to deceive Bernard du Ha, was by him cunningly deceived. (1)

1 The incidents of this story must have occurred subsequent to 1527. The secretary is doubtless John Frotté. We have failed to identify the Lieutenant referred to.—M. and Ed.

It chanced that when King Francis, first of the name, was in the city of Paris, and with him his sister, the Queen of Navarre, the latter had a secretary called John. He was not one of those who allow a good thing to lie on the ground for want of picking it up, and there was, accordingly, not a president or a councillor whom he did not know, and not a merchant or a rich man with whom he had not intercourse and correspondence.

At this time there also arrived in Paris a merchant of Bayonne, called Bernard du Ha, who, both on account of the nature of his commerce and because the Lieutenant for Criminal Affairs (2) was a countryman of his, was wont to address himself to that officer for counsel and assistance in the transaction of his business. The Queen of Navarre's secretary used also frequently to visit the Lieutenant as one who was a good servant to his master and mistress.

2 The Provost of Paris, who, in the King's name, administered justice at the Châtelet court, and upon whose sergeants fell the duty of arresting and imprisoning all vagabonds, criminals and disturbers of the peace, was assisted in his functions by three lieutenants, one for criminal affairs, one for civil affairs, and one for ordinary police duties.—Ed.

One feast-day the secretary went to the Lieutenant's house, and found both him and his wife abroad; but he very plainly heard Bernard du Ha teaching the serving-women to foot the Gascon dances to the sound of a viol or some other instrument. And when the secretary saw him, he would have had him believe that he was committing the greatest offence imaginable, and that if the Lieutenant and his wife knew of it they would be greatly displeased with him. And after setting the fear of this well before his eyes, until, indeed, the other begged him not to say anything about it, he asked—

"What will you give me if I keep silence?"

Bernard du Ha, who was by no means so much afraid as he seemed to be, saw that the secretary was trying to cozen him, and promised to give him a pasty of the best Basque ham (3) that he had ever eaten. The secretary was well pleased at this, and begged that he might have the pasty on the following Sunday after dinner, which was promised him.

3 So-called Bayonne ham is still held in repute in France. It comes really from Orthez and Salies in Beam.—D.

Relying upon this promise, he went to see a lady of Paris whom above all things he desired to marry, and said to her—

"On Sunday, mistress, I will come and sup with you, if such be your pleasure. But trouble not to provide aught save some good bread and wine, for I have so deceived a foolish fellow from Bayonne that all the rest will be at his expense; by my trickery you shall taste the best Basque ham that ever was eaten in Paris."

The lady believed his story, and called together two or three of the most honourable ladies of her neighbourhood, telling them that she would give them a new dish such as they had never tasted before.

When Sunday was come, the secretary went to look for his merchant, and finding him on the Pont-au-Change, (4) saluted him graciously and said—

"The devil take you, for the trouble you have given me to find you."

4 The oldest of the Paris bridges, spanning the Seine between the Châtelet and the Palais. Originally called the Grand-Pont, it acquired the name of Pont-au-Change through Louis VII. allowing the money-changers to build their houses and offices upon it in 1141.—Ed.

Bernard du Ha made reply that a good many men had taken more trouble than he without being rewarded in the end with such a dainty dish. So saying, he showed him the pasty, which he was carrying under his cloak, and which was big enough to feed an army. The secretary was so glad to see it that, although he had a very large and ugly mouth, he mincingly made it so small that one would not have thought him capable of biting the ham with it. He quickly took the pasty, and, without waiting for the merchant to go with him, went off with it to the lady, who was exceedingly eager to learn whether the fare of Gascony was as good as that of Paris.

When supper-time was come and they were eating their soup, the secretary said—

"Leave those savourless dishes alone, and let us taste this loveworthy whet for wine."

So saying, he opened the huge pasty, but, where he expected to find ham, he found such hardness that he could not thrust in his knife. After trying several times, it occurred to him that he had been deceived; and, indeed, he found 'twas a wooden shoe such as is worn in Gascony. It had a burnt stick for knuckle, and was powdered upon the top with iron rust and sweet-smelling spice.

If ever a man was abashed it was the secretary, not only because he had been deceived by the man whom he himself had thought to deceive, but also because he had deceived her to whom he had intended and thought to speak the truth. Moreover, he was much put out at having to content himself with soup for supper.

The ladies, who were well-nigh as vexed as he was, would have accused him of practising this deception had they not clearly seen by his face that he was more wroth than they.

After this slight supper, the secretary went away in great anger, intending, since Bernard du Ha had broken his promise, to break also his own. He therefore betook himself to the Lieutenant's house, resolved to say the worst he could about the said Bernard.

Quick as he went, however, Bernard was first afield and had already related the whole story to the Lieutenant, who, in passing sentence, told the secretary that he had now learnt to his cost what it was to deceive a Gascon, and this was all the comfort that the secretary got in his shame.

The same thing befalls many who, believing that they are exceedingly clever, forget themselves in their cleverness; wherefore we should never do unto others differently than we would have them do unto us.

"I can assure you," said Geburon, "that I have often known similar things to come to pass, and have seen men who were deemed rustic blockheads deceive very shrewd people. None can be more foolish than he who thinks himself shrewd, nor wiser than he who knows his own nothingness."

"Still," said Parlamente, "a man who knows that he knows nothing, knows something after all."

"Now," said Simontault, "for fear lest time should fail us for our discourse, I give my vote to Nomerfide, for I am sure that her rhetoric will keep us no long while."

"Well," she replied, "I will tell you a tale such as you desire.

"I am not surprised, ladies, that love should afford Princes the means of escaping from danger, for they are bred up in the midst of so many well-informed persons that I should marvel still more if they were ignorant of anything. But the smaller the intelligence the more clearly is the inventiveness of love displayed, and for this reason I will relate to you a trick played by a priest through the prompting of love alone. In all other matters he was so ignorant that he could scarcely read his mass."

[The Husbandman surprised by the Fall of the Winnowing Fan]

TALE XXIX

A parson, surprised by the sudden return of a husbandman with whose wife he was making good cheer, quickly devised a means for saving himself at the expense of the worthy man, who was never any the wiser. (1)

1 Etienne brings this story into his Apologie pour Hérodote, ch xv.—B. J.

At a village called Carrelles, (2) in the county of Maine, there dwelt a rich husbandman who in his old age had married a fair young wife. She bore him no children, but consoled herself for this disappointment with several lovers.

2 Carrelles is at six leagues from Mayenne, in the canton of Gorron. Margaret's first husband, the Duke of Alençon, held various fiefs in this part of Maine, which would account for the incident related in the story coming to her knowledge.—M. and Ed.

When gentlemen and persons of consequence failed her, she turned as a last resource to the Church, and took for companion in her sin him who could absolve her of it—that is to say, the parson, who often came to visit his pet ewe. The husband, who was dull and old, had no suspicion of the truth; but, as he was a stern and sturdy man, his wife played her game as secretly as she was able, fearing that, if it came to her husband's knowledge, he would kill her.

One day when he was abroad, his wife, thinking that he would not soon return, sent for his reverence the parson, who came to confess her; and while they were making good cheer together, her husband arrived, and this so suddenly that the priest had not the time to escape out of the house.

Looking about for a means of concealment, he mounted by the woman's advice into a loft, and covered the trap-door through which he passed with a winnowing fan.

The husband entered the house, and his wife, fearing lest he might suspect something, regaled him exceedingly well at dinner, never sparing the liquor, of which he drank so much, that, being moreover wearied with his work in the fields, he at last fell asleep in his chair in front of the fire.

The parson, tired with waiting so long in the loft, and hearing no noise in the room beneath, leaned over the trap-door, and, stretching out his neck as far as he was able, perceived the goodman to be asleep. However, whilst he was looking at him, he leaned by mischance so heavily upon the fan, that both fan and himself tumbled down by the side of the sleeper. The latter awoke at the noise, but the priest was on his feet before the other had perceived him, and said—

"There is your fan, my friend, and many thanks to you for it."

With these words he took to flight. The poor husbandman was in utter bewilderment.

"What is this?" he asked of his wife. "'Tis your fan, sweetheart," she replied, "which the parson had borrowed, and has just brought back."

Thereupon in a grumbling fashion the goodman rejoined—

"'Tis a rude way of returning what one has borrowed, for I thought the house was coming down."

In this way did the parson save himself at the expense of the goodman, who discovered nothing to find fault with except the rudeness with which the fan had been returned.

"The master, ladies, whom the parson served, saved him that time so that he might afterwards possess and torment him the longer."

"Do not imagine," said Geburon, "that simple folk are more devoid of craft than we are; (3) nay, they have a still larger share. Consider the thieves and murderers and sorcerers and coiners, and all the people of that sort, whose brains are never at rest; they are all poor and of the class of artisans."

"I do not think it strange," said Parlamente, "that they should have more craft than others, but rather that love should torment them amid their many toils, and that so gentle a passion should lodge in hearts so base."

"Madam," replied Saffredent, "you know what Master Jehan de Mehun has said—

"Those clad in drugget love no less

Than those that wear a silken dress." (4)

3 In MS. No. 1520 this passage runs—"that simple and humble people are," &c.—L.

4 This is a free rendering of lines 4925-6 of Méon's edition of the Roman de la Rose:—

"Aussy bien sont amourettes
Soubz bureau que soubz brunettes."

Bureau, the same as dure, is a kind of drugget; brunette was a silken stuff very fashionable among the French lords and ladies at the time of St. Louis. It was doubtless of a brown hue.—B, J. and M.

Moreover, the love of which the tale speaks is not such as makes one carry harness; for, while poor folk lack our possessions and honours, on the other hand they have their natural advantages more at their convenience than we. Their fare is not so dainty as ours, but their appetites are keener, and they live better on coarse bread than we do on delicacies. Their beds are not so handsome or so well appointed as ours, but their sleep is sounder and their rest less broken. They have no ladies pranked out and painted like those whom we idolise, but they take their pleasure oftener than we, without fear of telltale tongues, save those of the beasts and birds that see them. What we have they lack, and what we lack they possess in abundance."

"I pray you," said Nomerfide, "let us now have done with this peasant and his wife, and let us finish the day's entertainment before vespers. 'Tis Hircan shall bring it to an end."

"Truly," said he, "I have kept in reserve as strange and pitiful a tale as ever you heard. And although it grieves me greatly to relate anything to the discredit of a lady, knowing, as I do, that men are malicious enough to blame the whole sex for the fault of one, yet the strangeness of the story prompts me to lay aside my fear. Perhaps, also, the discovery of one woman's ignorance will make others wiser. And so I will fearlessly tell you the following tale."

[The Young Gentleman embracing his Mother]

TALE XXX

A young gentleman, of from fourteen to fifteen years of age, thought to lie with one of his mother's maids, but lay with his mother herself; and she, in consequence thereof, was, nine months afterwards, brought to bed of a daughter, who, twelve or thirteen years later, was wedded by the son; he being ignorant that she was his daughter and sister, and she, that he was her father and brother.(1)

In the time of King Louis the Twelfth, the Legate at Avignon being then a scion of the house of Amboise, nephew to George, Legate of France, (2) there lived in the land of Languedoc a lady who had an income of more than four thousand ducats a year, and whose name I shall not mention for the love I bear her kinsfolk.

1 This story is based on an ancient popular tradition common to many parts of France, and some particulars of which, with a list of similar tales in various European languages, will be found in the Appendix, D.—En.

2 The Papal Legate in France here alluded to is the famous George, Cardinal d'Amboise, favourite minister of Louis XII. His nephew, the Legate at Avignon, is Louis d'Amboise, fourth son of Peter d'Amboise, Lord of Chaumont, and brother of the Grand-Master of Chaumont. Louis d'Amboise became bishop of Albi, and lieutenant-general of the King of France in Burgundy, Languedoc and Roussillon, and played an important part in the public affairs of his time. He died in 1505.—See Gallia Christiana, vol. i. p. 34.—L. and R. J.

While still very young, she was left a widow with one son; and, both by reason of her regret for her husband and her love for her child, she determined never to marry again. To avoid all opportunity of doing so, she had fellowship only with the devout, for she imagined that opportunity makes the sin, not knowing that sin will devise the opportunity.

This young widow, then, gave herself up wholly to the service of God, and shunned all worldly assemblies so completely that she scrupled to be present at a wedding, or even to listen to the organs playing in a church. When her son was come to the age of seven years, she chose for his schoolmaster a man of holy life, so that he might be trained up in all piety and devotion.

When the son was reaching the age of fourteen or fifteen, Nature, who is a very secret schoolmaster, finding him in good condition and very idle, taught him a different lesson to any he had learned from his tutor. He began to look at and desire such things as he deemed beautiful, and among others a maiden who slept in his mother's room. No one had any suspicion of this, for he was looked upon as a mere child, and, moreover, in that household nothing save godly talk was ever heard.

This young gallant, however, began secretly soliciting the girl, who complained of it to her mistress. The latter had so much love for her son and so high an opinion of him, that she thought the girl spoke as she did in order to make her hate him; but, being strongly urged by the other, she at last said—

"I shall find out whether it is true, and will punish him if it be as you say. But if, on the other hand, you are bringing an untruthful accusation against him, you shall suffer for it."

Then, in order to test the matter, she bade the girl make an appointment with her son that he might come and lie with her at midnight, in the bed in which she slept alone, beside the door of his mother's room.

The maid obeyed her mistress, who, when night came, took the girl's place, resolved, if the story were true, to punish her son so severely that he would never again lie with a woman without remembering it.

While she was thinking thus wrathfully, her son came and got into the bed, but although she beheld him do so, she could not yet believe that he meditated any unworthy deed. She therefore refrained from speaking to him until he had given her some token of his evil intent, for no trifling matters could persuade her that his desire was actually a criminal one. Her patience, however, was tried so long, and her nature proved so frail that, forgetting her motherhood, her anger became transformed into an abominable delight. And just as water that has been restrained by force rushes onward with the greater vehemence when it is released, so was it with this unhappy lady who had so prided herself on the constraint she had put upon her body. After taking the first step downwards to dishonour, she suddenly found herself at the bottom, and thus that night she became pregnant by him whom she had thought to restrain from acting in similar fashion towards another.

No sooner was the sin accomplished than such remorse of conscience began to torment her as filled the whole of her after-life with repentance. And so keen was it at the first, that she rose from beside her son—who still thought that she was the maid—and entered a closet, where, dwelling upon the goodness of her intention and the wickedness of its execution, she spent the whole night alone in tears and lamentation.

But instead of humbling herself, and recognising the powerlessness of our flesh, without God's assistance, to work anything but sin, she sought by her own tears and efforts to atone for the past, and by her own prudence to avoid mischief in the future, always ascribing her sin to circumstances and not to wickedness, for which there is no remedy save the grace of God. Accordingly she sought to act so as never again to fall into such wrongdoing; and as though there were but one sin that brought damnation in its train, she put forth all her strength to shun that sin alone.

But the roots of pride, which acts of sin ought rather to destroy, grew stronger and stronger within her, so that in avoiding one evil she wrought many others. Early on the morrow, as soon as it was light, she sent for her son's preceptor, and said—

"My son is beginning to grow up, it is time to send him from home. I have a kinsman, Captain Monteson, (3) who is beyond the mountains with my lord the Grand-Master of Chaumont, and he will be very glad to admit him into his company. Take him, therefore, without delay, and to spare me the pain of parting do not let him come to bid me farewell."

3 Monteson was one of the bravest captains of his time; as the comrade of Bayard, he greatly distinguished himself by his intrepidity in Louis XII.'s Italian campaigns. Some particulars concerning him will be found in M. Lacroix's edition of Les Chroniques de Jean d'Anton.—B. J. Respecting the Grand-Master of Chaumont, also mentioned above, see ante, vol ii., notes to Tale XIV.

So saying, she gave him money for the journey, and that very morning sent the young man away, he being right glad of this, for, after enjoying his sweetheart, he asked nothing better than to set off to the wars.

The lady continued for a great while in deep sadness and melancholy, and, but for the fear of God, had many a time longed that the unhappy fruit of her womb might perish. She feigned sickness, in order that she might wear a cloak and so conceal her condition; and having a bastard brother, in whom she had more trust than in any one else, and upon whom she had conferred many benefits, she sent for him when the time of her confinement was drawing nigh, told him her condition (but without mentioning her son's part in it), and besought him to help her save her honour. This he did, and, a few days before the time when she expected to be delivered, he begged her to try a change of air and remove to his house, where she would recover her health more quickly than at home. Thither she went with but a very small following, and found there a midwife who had been summoned as for her brother's wife, and who one night, without recognising her, delivered her of a fine little girl. The gentleman gave the child to a nurse, and caused it to be cared for as his own.

After continuing there for a month, the lady returned in sound health to her own house, where she lived more austerely than ever in fasts and disciplines. But when her son was grown up, he sent to beg his mother's permission to return home, as there was at that time no war in Italy. She, fearing lest she should fall again into the same misfortune, would not at first allow him, but he urged her so earnestly that at last she could find no reason for refusing him. However, she instructed him that he was not to appear before her until he was married to a woman whom he dearly loved; but to whose fortune he need give no heed, for it would suffice if she were of gentle birth.

Meanwhile her bastard brother, finding that the daughter left in his charge had grown to be a tall maiden of perfect beauty, resolved to place her in some distant household where she would not be known, and by the mother's advice she was given to Catherine, Queen of Navarre. (4) The maiden thus came to the age of twelve or thirteen years, and was so beautiful and virtuous that the Queen of Navarre had great friendship for her, and much desired to marry her to one of wealth and station. Being poor, however, she found no husband, though she had lovers enough and to spare.

4 This is Catherine, daughter of Gaston and sister of Francis Phoebus de Foix. On her brother's death, in 1483, she became Queen of Navarre, Duchess of Nemours and Countess of Foix and Bigorre, and in the following year espoused John, eldest son of Alan, Sire d'Albret. Catherine at this time was fourteen years old, and her husband, who by the marriage became King of Navarre, was only one year her senior. Their title to the crown was disputed by a dozen pretenders, for several years they exercised but a precarious authority, and eventually, in July 1512, Ferdinand the Catholic despatched the Duke of Alva to besiege Pamplona. On the fourth day of the siege John and Catherine succeeded in escaping from their capital, which, three days later, surrendered. Ferdinand, having sworn to maintain the fueros, was thereupon acknowledged as sovereign. However, it was only in 1516 that the former rulers were expelled from Navarrese territory. "Had I been Don Juan and you Donna Catherine," said the Queen to her pusillanimous husband, as they crossed the Pyrenees, "we should not have lost our kingdom." From this time forward the d'Albrets, like their successors the Bourbons, were sovereigns of Navarre in name only, for an attempt made in 1521 to reconquer the kingdom resulted in total failure, and their dominions were thenceforth confined to Beam, Bigorre, and Foix on the French side of the Pyrenees. Queen Catherine died in 1517, aged 47, leaving several children, the eldest of whom was Henry, Queen Margaret's second husband.—M., B. J., D. and Ed.

Now it happened one day that the gentleman who was her unknown father came to the house of the Queen of Navarre on his way back from beyond the mountains, and as soon as he had set eyes on his daughter he fell in love with her, and having license from his mother to marry any woman that might please him, he only inquired whether she was of gentle birth, and, hearing that she was, asked her of the Queen in marriage. The Queen willingly consented, for she knew that the gentleman was not only rich and handsome, but worshipful to boot.

When the marriage had been consummated, the gentleman again wrote to his mother, saying that she could no longer close her doors against him, since he was bringing with him as fair a daughter-in-law as she could desire. The lady inquired to whom he had allied himself, and found that it was to none other than their own daughter. Thereupon she fell into such exceeding sorrow that she nearly came by a sudden death, seeing that the more she had striven to hinder her misfortune, the greater had it thereby become.

Not knowing what else to do, she went to the Legate of Avignon, to whom she confessed the enormity of her sin, at the same time asking his counsel as to how she ought to act. The Legate, to satisfy his conscience, sent for several doctors of theology, and laid the matter before them, without, however, mentioning any names; and their advice was that the lady should say nothing to her children, for they, being in ignorance, had committed no sin, but that she herself should continue doing penance all her life without allowing it to become known.

Accordingly, the unhappy lady returned home, where not long afterwards her son and daughter-in-law arrived. And they loved each other so much that never were there husband and wife more loving, nor yet more resembling each other; for she was his daughter, his sister and his wife, while he was her father, her brother and her husband. And this exceeding love between them continued always; and the unhappy and deeply penitent lady could never see them in dalliance together without going apart to weep.

"You see, ladies, what befalls those who think that by their own strength and virtue they may subdue Love and Nature and all the faculties that God has given them. It were better to recognise their own weakness, and instead of running a-tilt against such an adversary, to betake themselves to Him who is their true Friend, saying to Him in the words of the Psalmist, 'Lord, I am afflicted very much; answer Thou for me.'" (5)

5 We have failed to find this sentence in the Psalms. Probably the reference is to Isaiah xxxviii. 14, "O Lord, I am oppressed; undertake for me."—Eu.

"It were impossible," said Oisille "to hear a stranger story than this. Methinks every man and woman should bend low in the fear of God, seeing that in spite of a good intention so much mischief came to pass."

"You may be sure," said Parlamente, "that the first step a man takes in self-reliance, removes him so far from reliance upon God."

"A man is wise," said Geburon, "when he knows himself to be his greatest enemy, and holds his own wishes and counsels in suspicion."

"Albeit the motive might seem to be a good and holy one," said Longarine, "there were surely none, howsoever worthy in appearance, that should induce a woman to lie beside a man, whatever the kinship between them, for fire and tow may not safely come together."

"Without question," said Ennasuite, "she must have been some self-sufficient fool, who, in her friar-like dreaming, deemed herself so saintly as to be incapable of sin, just as many of the Friars would have us believe that we can become, merely by our own efforts, which is an exceeding great error."

"Is it possible, Longarine," asked Oisille, "that there are people foolish enough to hold such an opinion?"

"They go further than that," replied Longarine. "They say that we ought to accustom ourselves to the virtue of chastity; and in order to try their strength they speak with the prettiest women they can find and whom they like best, and by kissing and touching them essay whether their fleshly nature be wholly dead. When they find themselves stirred by such pleasure, they desist, and have recourse to fasts and grievous discipline. Then, when they have so far mortified their flesh that neither speech nor kiss has power to move them, they make trial of the supreme temptation, that, namely, of lying together and embracing without any lustfulness. (6) But for one who has escaped, so many have come to mischief, that the Archbishop of Milan, where this religious practice used to be carried on, (7) was obliged to separate them and place the women in convents and the men in monasteries."

6 Robert d'Arbrissel, the founder of the abbey of Fontevrault (see ante, p. 74), was accused of this practice.—See the article Fontevraud in Desoer's edition of Bayle's Dictionary, vi. 508, 519.—M.

7 Queen Margaret possibly refers to some incidents which occurred at Milan in the early part of the fourteenth century, when Matteo and Galeazzo Visconti ruled the city. In Signor Tullio Dandolo's work, Sui xxiii. libri delta Histories Patrice di Giuseppe Ripamonti ragionamento (Milano, 1856, pp. 52-60), will be found the story of a woman of the people, Guglielmina, and her accomplice, Andrea Saramita, who under some religious pretext founded a secret society of females. The debauchery practised by its members being discovered, Saramita was burnt alive, and Guglielmina's bones were disinterred and thrown into the fire. The Bishop of Milan at this time (1296-1308) was Francesco Fontana.—M.

"Truly," said Geburon, "it were the extremity of folly to seek to become sinless by one's own efforts, and at the same time to seek out opportunities for sin."

"There are some," said Saffredent, "who do the very opposite, and flee opportunities for sin as carefully as they are able; nevertheless, concupiscence pursues them. Thus the good Saint Jerome, after scourging and hiding himself in the desert, confessed that he could not escape from the fire that consumed his marrow. We ought, therefore, to recommend ourselves to God, for unless He uphold us by His power, we are greatly prone to fall."

"You do not notice what I do," said Hircan. "While we were telling our stories, the monks behind the hedge here heard nothing of the vesper-bell; whereas, now that we have begun to speak about God, they have taken themselves off, and are at this moment ringing the second bell."

"We shall do well to follow them," said Oisille, "and praise God for enabling us to spend this day in the happiest manner imaginable."

Hereat they rose and went to the church, where they piously heard vespers; after which they went to supper, discussing the discourses they had heard, and calling to mind divers adventures that had come to pass in their own day, in order to determine which of them were worthy to be recounted. And after spending the whole evening in gladness, they betook themselves to their gentle rest, hoping on the morrow to continue this pastime which was so agreeable to them.

And so was the Third Day brought to an end.

APPENDIX

A. (Tale XX.)

Brantôme alludes as follows to this tale, in the Fourth Discourse of his *Vies des Dames Galantes*:—

"I knew a great lady whose plumpness was the subject of general talk both whilst she was a maid and when she became a wife, but she happened to lose her husband, and gave way to such extreme grief that she became as dry as a stick. Still she did not cease to enjoy herself to her heart's content, with the assistance of one of her secretaries, and even so it is said of her cook. Nevertheless, she did not regain her plumpness, albeit the said cook, who was all grease and fat, should as it seems to me have made her stout again. Whilst she thus amused herself with one and another of her varlets, she affected more prudery and chastity than any other lady of the Court, having none but words of virtue on her lips, speaking ill of all other women and finding something to be censured in each of them. Very similar to this one was that great lady of Dauphiné who is mentioned in the Hundred Tales of the Queen of Navarre, and who was found, lying on the grass with her stableman or muleteer, by a gentleman who was in love with her to distraction. On finding her thus, however, he was speedily cured of his love-sickness.

"I have read in an old romance about John de Saintré, printed in black-letter, that the late King John brought him up as a page. In the old times it was usual for great personages to send their pages about with messages, as is indeed done nowadays, but at that time they journeyed anywhere across country, on horseback. In fact, I have heard our fathers say that pages were often sent on little embassies, for very often a matter would be settled and expense saved by merely despatching a page with a horse and a piece of silver. This little Jehan de Saintré, as he was long called, was a great favourite with his master King John, for he was full of wit, and it often happened that he was sent with messages to his [the King's?] sister, who was then a widow, though of whom the book does not say. This lady fell in love with him after several messages that he had delivered to her, and one day finding him alone, she engaged him in converse, and, according to the usual practice of ladies when they wish to engage any one in a love attack, she began to ask him if he were in love with any lady of the Court, and which one pleased him the most. This little John de Saintre, who had never even so much as thought of love, told her that he cared for none at the Court as yet, whereupon she mentioned several other ladies to him, and asked him whether he thought of them. 'Still less,' replied he.... Thereupon the lady, seeing that the young fellow was of good appearance, told him that she would give him a mistress who would love him tenderly if he would serve her well, and whilst he stood there feeling greatly ashamed, she made him promise that he would keep the matter secret, and finally declared to him that she herself wished to be his lady and lover, for at that time the word 'mistress' was not yet used. The young page was vastly astonished, thinking that the lady was joking, or wished to deceive him or to have him whipped. However, she soon showed him so many signs of the fire and fever of love, saying to him that she wished to tutor him and make a man of him, that he at last realised that it was not a jest. Their love lasted for a long time, both whilst he was a page and afterwards, until at length he had to go upon a long journey, when she replaced him by a big, fat abbot. This is the same story that one finds in the *Nouvelles du Monde Advantureux* by a valet of the Queen of Navarre [Antoine de St. Denis], in which one sees the abbot insult this same John de Saintré who was so brave and valiant, and who right speedily and liberally paid back my lord the abbot in his own coin.... So you see it is no new thing for ladies to love pages. What inclinations some women have, they will willingly take any number of lovers but they want no husband! All this is through love of liberty, which they deem such a pleasant thing. It seems to them as though they were in Paradise when they are not under a husband's rule. They have a fine dowry and spend it thriftily, they have all their household affairs in hand, receive their income, everything passing through their hands; and instead of being servants they are mistresses, select their own pleasures and favourites, and amuse themselves as much as they like."—Lalanne's *OEuvres de Brantôme*, vol. xi. pp. 703-6.

B. (Tale XXV.)

Baron Jerome Pichon's elucidations of this story, as given by him in the *Mélanges de la Société des Bibliophiles Français*, 1866, may be thus summarised:—

The advocate referred to in the tale is James Disome, who Mézeray declares was the *first* to introduce Letters to the bar, though this, to my mind, is a very hazardous assertion. Disome was twice married. His first wife, Mary de Rueil, died Sept. 17, 1511, and was buried at the Cordeliers church; he afterwards espoused Jane Lecoq, daughter of John Lecoq, Counsellor of the Paris Parliament, who held the fiefs of Goupillières, Corbeville and Les Porcherons, where he possessed a handsome château, a view of which has been engraved by Israel Silvestre. John Lecoq's wife was Magdalen Bochart, who belonged like her husband to an illustrious family of lawyers and judges. Their daughter Jane, who is the heroine of the tale, must have been married to James Disome not very long after the death of the latter's first wife, for her intrigue with Francis I. originated prior to his accession to the throne (1515). This is proved by the tale, in which Disome is spoken of as being the young prince's advocate. Now none but the Procurors and Advocates-General were counsel to the Crown, and Disome held neither of those offices. He was undoubtedly advocate to Francis as Duke de Valois, and, from certain allusions in the tale, it may be conjectured that he had been advocate to Francis's father, the Count of Angoulême.

When Francis ascended the throne his intrigue with Jane Disome was already notorious, as is proved by this extract, under date 1515, from the *Journal d'un Bourgeois de Paris*: "About this time whilst the King was in Paris, there was a priest called Mons. Cruche, a great buffoon, who a little time before with several others had publicly performed in certain entertainments and novelties' (*sic*) on scaffolds upon the Place Maubert, there being in turn jest, sermon, morality and farce; and in the morality appeared several lords taking their cloth of gold to the tomb and carrying their lands upon their shoulders into the other world. And in the farce came Monsieur Cruche with his companions, who had a lantern by which all sorts of things were seen, and among others a hen feeding under a salamander, (1) and this hen carried something on her back which would suffice to kill ten men (*dix hommes, i.e.,* Disome).

1 The salamander was Francis I.'s device.

The interpretation of this was that the King loved and enjoyed a woman of Paris, who was the daughter of a counsellor of the Court of Parliament, named Monsieur le Coq. And she was married to an advocate at the bar of Parliament, a very skilful man, named Monsieur James Disome, who was possessed of much property which the King confiscated. Soon afterwards the King sent eight or ten of his principal gentlemen to sup at the sign of the Castle in the Rue de la Juiverie, and thither, under the false pretence of making him play the said farce, was summoned Messire Cruche, who came in the evening, by torch-light, and was constrained to play the farce by the said gentlemen. But thereupon, at the very beginning, he was stripped to his shirt, and wonderfully well whipped with straps until he was in a state of the utmost wretchedness. At the end there was a sack all ready to put him in, that he might be thrown from the window, and then carried to the river; and this would assuredly have come to pass had not the poor man cried out very loudly and shown them the tonsure on his head. And all these things were done, so it was owned, on the King's behalf."

It is probable that this intrigue between the King and Jane Disome ceased soon after the former's accession; at all events Francis did not evince much indulgence for the man whose wife he had seduced. Under date April, 1518, the Journal dun Bourgeois de Paris mentions the arrest of several advocates and others for daring to discuss the question of the Pragmatic Sanction. Disome was implicated in the matter but appears to have escaped for a time; however in September of that year we find him detained at Orleans and subjected to the interrogatories of various royal Commissioners. The affair was then adjourned till the following year, when no further mention is made of it.

Disome died prior to 1521, for in September of that year we find his wife remarried to Peter Perdrier, Lord of Baubigny, notary and secretary to the King, and subsequently clerk of the council to the city of Paris. Perdrier was a man of considerable means; for when the King raised a forced loan of silver plate in September 1521, we find him taxed to the amount of forty marcs of silver (26 1/2 lbs. troy); or only ten *marcs* less than each counsellor of Parliament was required to contribute. Five and twenty years later, he lost his wife Jane, the curious record of whose death runs as follows: "The year one thousand five hundred forty-six, after Easter, at her house (hôtel) Rue de la Parcheminerie, called Rue des Blancs-Manteaux, died the late Demoiselle Jane Lecoq, daughter of Master John Lecoq, Counsellor of the Court of Parliament, deceased; in her lifetime wife of noble Master Peter Perdrier, Lord of Baubigny, &c, and previously wife of the late Master James Disome, in his lifetime advocate at the Court of Parliament and Lord of Cernay in Beauvaisis; and the said Demoiselle Jane Lecoq (2) is here—buried with her father and mother, and departed this life on the 23rd day of April 1546. Pray ye God for her soul."

2 *The church of the Celestines.*

Less than a twelvemonth afterwards King Francis followed his whilom mistress to the tomb. She left by Peter Perdrier a son named John, Lord of Baubigny, who in 1558 married Anne de St. Simon, grand-aunt of the author of the Memoirs. John Perdrier was possibly the Baubigny who killed Marshal de St. André at the battle of Dreux in 1562.

Such is Baron Pichon's account of Jane Lecoq and her husbands. We have now to turn to an often-quoted passage of the *Diverses Leçons* of Louis Guyon, sieur de la Nauthe, a physician of some repute in his time, but whose book it should be observed was not issued till 1610, or more than half-a-century subsequent to King Francis I.'s death. La Nauthe writes as follows:—

"Francis I. became enamoured of a woman of great beauty and grace, the wife of an advocate of Paris, whom I will not name, for he has left children in possession of high estate and good repute; and this lady would not yield to the King, but on the contrary repulsed him with many harsh words, whereat the King was sorely vexed. And certain courtiers and royal princes who knew of the matter told the King that he might take her authoritatively and by virtue of his royalty, and one of them even went and told this to the lady, who repeated it to her husband. The advocate clearly perceived that he and his wife must needs quit the kingdom, and that he would indeed find it hard to escape without obeying. Finally the husband gave his wife leave to comply with the King's desire, and in order that he might be no hindrance in the matter, he pretended to have business in the country for eight or ten days; during which time, however, he remained concealed in Paris, frequenting the brothels and trying to contract a venereal disease in order to give it to his wife, so that the King might catch it from her; and he speedily found what he sought, and infected his wife and she the King, who gave it to several other women, whom he kept, and could never get thoroughly cured, for all the rest of his life he remained unhealthy, sad, peevish and inaccessible."

Brantôme, it may be mentioned, also speaks of the King contracting a complaint through his gallantries, and declares that it shortened his life, but he mentions no woman by name, and does not tell the story of the advocate's wife. It will have been observed in the extract we have quoted that Guyon de la Nauthe says that the advocate had left children "in possession of high estate and good repute." Disome, however, had no children either by his first or his second wife. The question therefore arises whether La Nauthe is not referring to another advocate, for instance Le Féron, husband of La belle Féronnière. These would appear to have left posterity (see *Catalogue de tous les Conseillers du Parlement de Paris*, pp. 120-2-3, and Blanchard's *les Présidents à mortier du Parlement de Paris, etc.*, 1647, 8vo). But it should be borne in mind that the Féronnière intrigue is purely traditional. The modern writers who speak of it content themselves with referring to Mézeray, a very doubtful authority at most times, and who did not write, it should be remembered, till the middle of the seventeenth century, his *Abrégé Chronologique* being first published in 1667. Moreover, when we come to consult him we find that he merely makes a passing allusion to La Féronnière, and even this is of the most dubious kind. Here are his words: "In 1538 the King had a long illness at Compiègne, caused by an ulcer.... He was cured at the time, but died [of it?] nine years later. *I have sometimes heard say*(!) that he caught this disease from La belle Féronnière."

Against this we have to set the express statement of Louise of Savoy, who writes in her journal, under date 1512, that her son (born in 1494) had already and at an early age had a complaint *en secrete nature*. Now this was long before the belle Féronnière was ever heard of, and further it was prior to the intrigue with Jane Disome, who, by Queen Margaret's showing, did not meet with "the young prince" until she had been married some time and was in despair of having children by her husband. The latter had lost his first wife late in 1511, and it is unlikely that he married Jane Lecoq until after some months of widowhood. To our thinking Prince Francis would have appeared upon the scene in or about 1514, his intrigue culminating in the scandal of the following year, in which Mons. Cruche played so conspicuous a part. With reference to the complaint from which King Francis is alleged to have suffered, one must not overlook the statement of a contemporary, Cardinal d'Armagnac, who, writing less than a year before the King's death, declares that Francis enjoys as good health as any man in his kingdom (Genin's *Lettres de Marguerite*, 1841, p. 473). Cardinal d'Armagnac's intimacy with the King enabled him to speak authoritatively, and his statement refutes the assertions of Brantôme, Guyon de la Nauthe and Mézeray, besides tending to the conclusion that the youthful complaint mentioned by Louise of Savoy was merely a passing disorder.—Ed.

C. (Tale XXVI.)

Brantome mentions this tale in both the First and the Fourth Discourse of his *Dames Galantes*. In the former, after contending that all women are naturally inclined to vice—a view which he borrows from the *Roman de la Rose*, and which Pope afterwards re-echoed in the familiar line, "Every woman is at heart a rake"—he proceeds to speak of those who overcome their inclinations and remain virtuous:—

"Of this," says he, "we have a very fine story in the Hundred Tales of the Queen of Navarre; the one in which that worthy Lady of Pampeluna, vicious at heart and by inclination, burning too with love for that handsome Prince, Monsieur d'Avannes, preferred to die consumed by the fire that possessed her rather than seek a remedy for it, as she herself declared in her last words on her deathbed. This worshipful and beautiful lady dealt herself death most iniquitously and unjustly; and as I once heard a worthy man and worthy lady say of this very passage, she did really offend against God, since it was in her power to deliver herself from death; whereas in seeking it and advancing it as she did, she really killed herself. And thus have done many similar to her, who by excessive continence and abstinence have brought about the destruction both of their souls and bodies."—Lalanne's *OEuvres de Brantôme*, vol. ix. pp. 209-n.

In the Fourth Discourse of his work, Brantôme mentions the case of a "fresh and plump" lady of high repute, who, through love-sickness for one of her admirers, so wasted away that she became seriously alarmed, and for fear of worse resolved to satisfy her passion, whereupon she became "plump and beautiful as she had been before."

"I have heard speak," adds Brantôme, "of another very great lady, of very joyous humour, and great wit, who fell ill and whose doctor told her that she would never recover unless she yielded to the dictates of nature, whereupon she instantly rejoined: 'Well then, let it be so;' and she and the doctor did as they listed.... One day she said to him: 'It is said everywhere that you have relations with me; but that is all the same to me, since it keeps me in good health... and it shall continue so, as long as may be, since my health depends on it.' These two ladies in no wise resemble that worthy lady of Pampeluna, in the Queen of Navarre's Hundred Tales, who, as I have previously said, fell madly in love with Monsieur d'Avannes, but preferred to hide her flame and nurse it in her burning breast rather than forego her honour. And of this I have heard some worthy ladies and lords discourse, saying that she was a fool, caring but little for the salvation of her soul, since she dealt herself death, when it was in her power to drive death away, at very trifling cost."-Lalanne's *OEuvres de Brantôme,* vol. xi. pp. 542-5.

To these extracts we may add that the problem discussed by Brantôme, three hundred years ago, is much the same as that which has so largely occupied the attention of modern medical men, namely the great spread of nervous disease and melancholia among women, owing to the unnatural celibacy enforced upon them by the deficiency of husbands.—Ed.

D. (Tale XXX.)

Various French, English and Italian authors have written imitations of this tale, concerning which Dunlop writes as follows in his History of Fiction:—

"The plot of Bandello's thirty-fifth story is the same as that of Horace Walpole's comedy *The Mysterious Mother,* and of the Queen of Navarre's thirtieth tale. The earlier portion will be found also in Masuccio's twenty-third tale: but the second part, relating to the marriage, occurs only in Bandello's work and the *Heptameron.* It is not likely, however, that the French or the Italian novelist borrowed from one another. The tales of Bandello were first published in 1554, and as the Queen of Navarre died in 1549, it is improbable that she ever had an opportunity of seeing them. On the other hand, the work of the Queen was not printed till 1558, nine years after her death, so it is not likely that any part of it was copied by Bandello, whose tales had been edited some years before."

Walpole, it may be mentioned, denied having had any knowledge either of the *Heptameron* or of Bandello when he wrote *The Mysterious Mother,* which was suggested to him, he declared, by a tale he had heard when very young, of a lady who had waited on Archbishop Tillotson with a story similar to that which is told by Queen Margaret's heroine to the Legate of Avignon. According to Walpole, Tillotson's advice was identical with that given by the Legate.

Dunlop mentions that a tale of this character is given in Byshop's *Blossoms* (vol. xi.); and other authors whose writings contain similar stories are: Giovani Brevio, *Rime e Prose vulgari,* Roma, 1545 (Novella iv.); Desfontaine's *L'Inceste innocent, histoire véritable,* Paris, 1644 5 Tommaso Grappulo, or Grappolino, *Il Convito Borghesiano,* Londra, 1800 (Novella vii.);

Luther, *Colloquia Mens alia* (article on auricular confession); and Masuccio de Solerac, *Novellino*, Ginevra, 1765 (Novella xxiii.).

Curiously enough, Bandello declares that the story was related to him by a lady of Navarre (Queen Margaret?) as having occurred in that country, while Julio de Medrano, a Spanish author of the sixteenth century, asserts that it was told to him in the Bourbonnais as being actual fact, and that he positively saw the house where the lady's son and his wife resided; but on the other hand we find the tale related, in its broad lines, in *Amadis de Gaule* as being an old-time legend, and in proof of this, it figures in an ancient French poem of the life of St. Gregory, the MS. of which still exists at Tours, and was printed in 1854.

In support of the theory that the tale is based on actual fact, the following passage from Millin's *Antiquités Nationales* (vol. iii. f. xxviii. p. 6) is quoted—

"In the middle of the nave of the collégial church of Ecouis, in the cross aisle, was found a white marble slab on which was inscribed this epitaph:—

"Hore lies the child, here lies the father,
Here lies the sister, here lies the brother,
Here lie the wife and the husband,
Yet there are but two bodies here."

"The tradition is that a son of Madame d'Écouis had by his mother, without knowing her or being recognised by her, a daughter named Cecilia, whom he afterwards married in Lorraine, she then being in the service of the Duchess of Bar. Thus Cecilia was at one and the same time her husband's daughter, sister and wife. They were interred together in the same grave at Écouis in 1512."

According to Millin, a similar tradition will be found with variations in different parts of France. For instance, at the church of Alincourt, a village between Amiens and Abbeville, there was to be seen in Millin's time an epitaph running as follows:—

"Here lies the son, here lies the mother,
Here lies the daughter with the father;
Here lies the sister, here lies the brother,
Here lie the wife and the husband;
And there are only three bodies here."

Gaspard Meturas, it may be added, gives the same epitaph in his *Hortus Epitaphiomm Selectorum,* issued in 1648, but declares that it is to be found at Clermont in Auvergne—a long way from Amiens—and explains it by saying that the mother engendered her husband by intercourse with her own father; whence it follows that he was at the same time her husband, son and brother.—L. M. and Ed.